NOW

A NOVEL

OR

NEVER

A.J. BENNETT

Cover Art by Eden Crane Design
Editing by Heather Adkins and Allison Potter
Formatting by Eden Crane Design

Dedication

To anyone that's been in a bad relationship.

CHAPTER 1

Grayson was sick of her psycho jealous fiancé.

She twirled the small diamond ring on her finger, wondering why the hell she even said "yes" in the first place. Evening light barely filtered through the tiny window behind her as she sat on the couch, her back aching from bending over as she balanced her checkbook.

She collapsed onto the cushions and rubbed her face; maybe her palms could erase the image of woefully small numbers in her account—yet another example of bad decisions in her life.

The more she thought about it, the more she realized it was seriously past time for her to escape such a toxic relationship. She already gave the jackass three years of her life, not to mention her virginity. If she didn't get out soon, she would end up married and miserable.

No, thanks.

Grayson sat forward to tackle her never-ending list of receipts. As she picked up her pen, she heard the front door open. Josh stalked into the living room.

Speak of the devil, she thought irritably, tossing her pen down.

The blue eyes she used to adore were wild and his lean body tense. His blond hair was sticking up like he'd been running his hands through it. It was one of the many nervous habits that she used to think was sexy.

"You think you're so smart, don't you, Grayson?" he snapped, slamming the door shut with enough force to make the crappy clapboard walls of the apartment shake.

Just perfect, Grayson thought with a mix of fire and fear. *The neighbors will probably ask me if I am okay again. The pity in their eyes is always a great self-esteem booster.* The 8x10 picture of them at the beach, which hung on the wall next to the front door, crashed to the floor... again. *There has got to be some irony in there somewhere.*

Great. Now what did I do? Grayson took a deep breath, bracing herself for yet another confrontation. Why couldn't they make it through one day without a fight?

"I'm not in the mood to play games," she said wearily, crossing her arms over her chest. "What are you talking about this time?"

He strode across the room in his heavy boots— just another thing the downstairs neighbors liked to complain about on top of the yelling and slamming doors. Grayson tensed as he stopped at the edge of the couch. She didn't fight him when he snatched her arm and yanked her to her feet.

Their faces were only inches apart. She could feel his hot breath on her skin. It made her stomach turn.

"I saw you!" he yelled, shaking her roughly. His

usually handsome face twisted into something grotesque. "You're such a whore! I knew you couldn't keep your pants on."

Grayson inhaled sharply and jerked away from his grip. *Great, more bruises to hide.* He was always careful not to touch her face. Well, except for that one time. She had to come up with some lame excuse for a black eye, like the stereotypical "I ran into a door" justification, which of course, no one bought—especially not her twin sister.

"What exactly did you see me doing?" She bit back from saying what was really on her mind.

Josh grabbed her biceps once more and squeezed, his strong fingers digging in painfully. "You know what you did!"

Grayson rolled her eyes at him, trying to brush it off as nothing, even though her heart was pounding like a hummingbird on crack. Josh always accused Grayson of cheating on him. It wasn't like she hadn't been tempted to stray a time or two. She was only human after all, and he was a jackass. However, she was nothing but faithful to the jerk during the entire three years they'd been together.

Grayson kept her response calm. "I have no idea what you're talking about."

She tried to pull her arms away, but his grip was too strong. A vein pulsed on his forehead, and his face was an unnatural shade of red, an indication he was about to go into one of his rages. She knew from experience it was best to defuse the situation as quickly as possible.

"I've done nothing wrong," she went on evenly. "So there is nothing you could have seen."

He finally let her go. "At the bookstore today? Does

that jar your memory at all?"

What the hell was he talking about? She had been at the bookstore earlier, but what was bad about that? She always went there to study. She couldn't think of anything that she had done that would cause this reaction.

"What, are you stalking me now?" Grayson asked, temper starting to flare. *Deep breaths,* she told herself before going on. "Why didn't you come over and talk to me if you saw me in the bookstore?"

"You were too busy flirting with someone else." He glared at her, his hands clenched into fists by his side, making Grayson hope they would stay where they were and not take a journey to her body.

"You were laughing and tossing your hair over your shoulder. I saw everything." He even got theatrical acting out the scene of her crime. All she could see was fury in his eyes.

"Josh, this is really getting ridiculous." Grayson tried to think back to whom she'd talked to, but she wasn't there long that day. The café filled up quickly, and the noise level got too loud to concentrate, so she left.

"So you're still going to deny it?" Josh shook his head. "Caught in the act, and you're going to look me in the eye and lie?"

"There's nothing to lie about. If I was talking to anyone it was totally innocent."

"Innocent! You call giving someone your phone number innocent?"

Okay, clearly he was off his rocker this time. She'd never given anyone her number; she racked her brain for some sort of explanation. Then her eyes widened as she realized what he was talking about.

"I didn't give anyone my phone number. What you saw was me copying down the date on when a book is coming out by an author I like, period. That guy you saw works at the store. Go on, check my phone, and you'll see. It's in my calendar. You should know your way around my phone by now."

Josh grabbed her phone from the coffee table and started scrolling through it like a mad man. After a moment, he growled, "Who the hell is Charles?"

"He's my uncle. You asshole." Grayson reached for her phone. "You know what, Joshua? I can't do this anymore. I'm done. We're over."

Nevertheless, she wasn't fast enough. Before she even got near her phone, Josh knocked her hand away and shoved her. She stumbled backwards into the wall, arms flailing. Her head hit the drywall with a dull thud, and stars burst in her eyes. She felt herself slowly falling to the floor.

Something inside of Grayson snapped. She'd had enough. She scrambled away from him, putting distance between them as he stood watching her. She felt like a mouse waiting for the pissed-off cat to pounce.

"Get out!" she shrieked, struggling to her feet. She yanked the ring off her finger and threw it at him. "We are done!"

Josh charged her and grabbed her by the throat with his hand. He slammed her against the wall. "We're not done until I say we're done. Understand? Got me?"

Grayson couldn't breathe. Her feet kicked at the air, and all of her weight settled against his grasp on her throat. He had her pinned with one hand. As she clawed at his hand, desperate for air, she realized she

didn't have a prayer of winning against him. He was bigger and stronger.

She struggled to nod, tears running down her cheeks. She would have said anything to get his hands off her before he choked her to death.

Josh dropped her to the floor, and like it always did, the switch flipped back again. Her anger and determination disappeared in the wake of his abuse.

Pulling her knees to her chest, she wrapped her arms around them and willed herself to disappear. *If only life were that easy.*

"Grayson?" Josh's voice cracked as he fell to his knees in front of her. His hands were gentle now as they brushed over her arms and neck. She didn't meet his eyes, but she knew there would be tears there.

"Grayson, I'm sorry. Oh my God. I didn't mean it. I just get so crazy thinking about you with anyone else. It's only because I love you so much. Can you please forgive me?"

Grayson rubbed her neck, and then wiped the tears off her cheeks but didn't answer or look him in the eye.

He took her gently by the arms and helped her to her feet. His voice was hoarse in her ear as he embraced her. "Please don't leave me. I'll die without you." He kissed her forehead. "My life is not worth living without you."

As always, he sounded so sincere.

All she could think about was how much she hated him, and how terrified she was that she would become like one of the girls on an after-school special—killed by a jealous boyfriend. How had she allowed this to happen? She used to be so confident and happy. Josh had slowly stripped away the person she had been, and she hated herself for that almost as much as she hated him.

Grayson forced herself to return the embrace, if a little stiffly. "You need help, Josh."

"I know I do. I'll go to counseling. I promise. Just don't leave me," he pleaded, stepping back so he could put the full force of his gaze on her. "I'll do anything you want."

How many times had he uttered those exact same words over the years? Her shoulders slumped. Way too many times to remember.

When he kissed her, she was revolted by the feel and taste of him, but she didn't stop him. It always worked this way. A huge fight, followed by crazy make-up sex, and then everything would be fine...until the next argument.

Josh deepened the kiss, one hand curling around her waist as he pressed his hips into hers. He murmured, "I love you," as he pulled off her shirt. "You're so beautiful."

I can't do this anymore, Grayson thought, fighting the urge to retch when her bra hit the floor, and his hands moved to cup her breasts—hands that had only moments before been wrapped around her neck.

The same neck Josh's lips now trailed down as he unbuttoned her jeans. She closed her eyes, tears soaking her cheeks.

This is the last time he will touch me, she thought with determination. She would go through the motions to calm him down, and then she would run as fast as she could without looking back. That was the only way.

"I need you so much, Grayson," he murmured, sliding her jeans down over her hips until she was naked before him. His gaze drifted down, and he licked his lips. "I don't want anyone else looking at you or talking to you. If I had it my way, I'd keep you locked in the house all to myself."

Grayson hummed to appease him, rubbing her wet face on her arm as his head dipped to her breasts.

When Josh lifted her off the ground, it was as if she weighed nothing at all. Instinctively, she wrapped her legs around his waist, and he carried her to the bedroom.

Please just get it over with, Grayson prayed as the door shut.

Thankfully, he never lasted long after a fight.

CHAPTER 2

Josh took his normal after-sex nap. Listening to his annoying snoring, Grayson lay in bed—as far away from him as she could get without falling off—and devised her escape plan.

There wasn't a whole lot to it. Her plan was simple: get out, and do it quick. She'd never been the kind of girl to make plans; she usually just winged it, which got her into trouble a time or two. Josh, on the other hand, was methodical about everything.

She had no idea where she was going or what she would do when she got there. She just knew she had to go.

So this is what they mean when they say someone needs to hit "rock bottom." Tonight is the final straw that broke this camel's back.

She'd met Josh her first semester of college, in the food court. There were plenty of times since then she'd find herself wishing she never smiled at him. It had been stupid. Josh wasn't even a student and was there with his girlfriend, some tall, dark-haired girl who looked barely legal. Grayson caught sight of him where he lounged at the table as if he owned it, his blond hair, and tan skin making his blue eyes look like sapphires. They caught each other's gaze, shared a smile, and the rest was history.

Lying in bed beside his naked body, Grayson realized that sex was all there had ever been between them. Nothing deeper, even though they'd said *I love you.* It wasn't anything more than a sex-induced infatuation. If she had known about his insane jealous streak back then, she wouldn't have given him the time of day. She'd always read about women getting involved with abusive men and thought they were foolish. Yet, here she was, three years later, doing just that. She was ashamed and embarrassed that she'd allowed herself to become a statistic.

Live and learn, she told herself. As far as she was concerned, if she never got involved in another relationship, that would be fine. The thought of being alone was a satisfying one. She didn't need a man or anyone else for that matter.

There was no question. She had to leave.

Josh jerked awake, one foot kicking out into Grayson's shin. She bit her tongue as he rolled over and blinked at the large red numbers on the alarm clock. "Shit, I'm going to be late for work."

Grayson glared at his back, but smoothed her face immediately when he turned around and smiled at her.

He rubbed her thigh above the covers. "Hey. Fix me dinner, Ok?"

She nodded and tossed off the blankets.

As the bathroom door shut behind him, and the shower turned on, Grayson breathed a sigh of relief. He worked the night shift, so he wouldn't be back until three in the morning. That left plenty of time for her to make a break for it.

The kitchen filled with the strong scent of coffee brewing. She listened to him as he got ready. He was always thumping loudly around the bedroom. She put together a ham and cheese sandwich for him, making sure to use enough mayo, so he wouldn't get pissed. A Ziploc baggie full of potato chips and an apple went into his lunch bag, and she filled his thirty-two-ounce canister of coffee with coffee and sugar.

"That's my girl." She hadn't even heard him enter the kitchen. Josh kissed her on the cheek as he swiped the lunch bag and coffee. He twisted the cap and took a chug, then made a face. "Not enough sugar."

Grayson froze, adrenaline pumping. She'd already survived one outburst today; she really didn't want or need another.

He shrugged. "No big deal. I don't need a sugar crash anyway. See you when I get home. Keep the bed warm for me."

"Of course," Grayson said, working overtime to keep her voice steady as she walked him to the door.

They kissed good-bye. *For the last time,* Grayson promised herself. The door slammed shut behind him. *Good riddance.*

Excitement and fear bubbled up in her chest as she turned around for one last look. This place, with its stark white walls and black furniture, had never felt like home. Even though they'd shared it for the last two years, it was always Josh's place. Grayson was just another temporary decoration in his apartment and life.

Or a welcome mat, she thought bitterly. She hated this place and would gladly leave it behind.

Grayson jumped into motion.

She pulled her suitcase from the front closet where it was wedged beneath two years' worth of accumulated belongings. In the bedroom, she grabbed clothes at random: jeans, sweaters, T-shirts, and undergarments and shoved them all inside. Her entire wardrobe wouldn't fit in her suitcase, but she didn't care.

Taking her jewelry box off the dresser, she dumped the contents on top of her clothes, pausing as her small collection of rocks knocked together. Pushing her bras and underwear to the side, Grayson pulled out a translucent amethyst the size of her fist and held it tightly to her chest. She had collected stones since she was a child. Josh thought it was a stupid hobby, so she hid them away. He thought pretty much everything she liked or did was a waste of time.

My new place will be filled with crystals, she thought with a smile. A new beginning.

Tossing the amethyst back in the bag, she looked around to see what else she was missing. She hated to leave her books, but they were replaceable. Everything was replaceable, except for her life. And she knew if she didn't leave now, she just might lose that, too.

Now or never, she thought.

Grayson decided to go with now. Life was too short to be this miserable.

She pushed down on the suitcase and zipped it closed. With a thud, she dropped it to the floor and pulled out the handle, dragging it behind her.

Standing in the doorway to the dim bedroom, she looked one last time at the plaid maroon and green bedspread on the king-sized bed and the ugly carpet. Josh didn't want anything 'girly' in his place. It looked like a bachelor pad. The only things that showed Grayson's personality had been hidden away in her dresser for two long years.

She longed for her old bedroom where her mother had let her paint the walls and ceiling a burnt orange. She thought it looked like the Grand Canyon, her own little cave. All the furniture had been dark wood, and her crystals had been on prominent display.

Her new place would look like that.

In the living room, she grabbed her photo albums from the bookshelf and threw them in the backpack that held her laptop. She couldn't leave them behind when they held so many childhood memories.

From the TV stand, she grabbed two small picture frames—one of her with her twin sister, and the second of a couple of friends from school. By the light of the television, Grayson stared down at the picture of her friends. She used to be so close to her group of girlfriends, but Josh got jealous if she spent time with anyone else, so she pulled away from the friends that she once treasured more than anything. How could she have been so stupid?

I gave up so much of my life, what made me happy, for Josh. Grayson felt like such a fool.

Maybe she was the one that needed counseling. She slipped both frames in her backpack. Her psycho fiancé carried a gun, for crying out loud, and he had on more than one occasion threatened to kill her and then himself. Why hadn't she listened to her grandmother? Nanny had told her Josh was no good. Grayson had a feeling she was watching down from heaven, rooting for her to run.

One more stop in the kitchen, where she yanked a post-it note off the fridge and rummaged in the junk drawer for a pen.

She bit her lip. What words did you use to say good-bye to a man who'd consistently threatened and abused her?

Josh,

I can't do this anymore. Don't look for me. We're done. If you come near me again, I will have a restraining order on you so fast your head will spin.

G

Grayson slapped the note to the kitchen table next to a sticky circle of dried beer, took off the engagement ring, and set it on top of the note. He never really wanted to get married. The only reason he'd given her a ring was so everyone would know she was taken.

Talk about a warning sign. Grayson seriously wanted to smack herself on the head for missing all of these signs.

She shut off all the lights as she passed through the apartment, grabbed her bag and backpack, and opened the door.

The moonless, starless night sky seemed to stretch forever beyond the balcony. Grayson took a deep breath of dry, hot air that smelled her downstairs neighbor's flowers.

With one last look over her shoulder into the darkness she was leaving behind, Grayson pulled the door shut with a bang. She didn't bother to lock it, which would piss off Josh. He hated when she didn't lock the doors, or clean the dishes right after eating, or...hell, just about anything she did was wrong. She'd never been able to please him—except in the bedroom. The only place they had ever seemed to get along, and even that had lost its appeal long ago.

Grayson walked with purpose to the staircase. In 3C, she heard canned laughter from the television, and the usual smell of Thai food drifted through the door at 3E. If anyone heard her heavy footsteps on the shared balcony, no one came to the door or peeked through the curtains.

Just as well. Grayson didn't want long good-byes or sympathetic eyes from people she barely knew, but who knew what her life had been like in that apartment.

Her beat-up old Jeep waited in her parking spot, dusty and sun-worn. Grayson tossed her bags in the back before sliding in the driver's seat.

A slow smile spread across her face as she pulled out of the lot, signaling to turn left on the highway.

Goodbye, Arizona.

She didn't look back.

CHAPTER 3

Ten miles down the road, the smile on Grayson's face disappeared, replaced by absent-minded lip biting. Her eyes flicked between the road and the rearview mirror. Every glimpse she caught of her oval freckled face framed by unbrushed strawberry-blonde hair made her jump. She looked haunted or maybe like a crazy person.

What if he was watching her now? What if the set of headlights behind her Jeep was his Mustang? She wouldn't put anything past him. He was going to freak when he found out she left him.

Grayson's heart seized. She clenched the steering wheel and forced herself to take three big breaths, letting them out slowly and counting the seconds. She was being paranoid. Josh was at work.

Calm down, she willed herself. You can do this.

As if right on cue, her phone rang. *You Give Love a Bad Name by Bon Jovi*— Josh's ring tone. Her twin sister had swapped the ring tones on her last visit, over six months ago. She looked down at the illuminated screen and grimaced. Nothing out of the ordinary. He always called to check up on her. It didn't mean he'd gone home early.

He doesn't know.

She stared at the phone as it vibrated in the cup holder, dancing in a circle around the edge like a living thing. Should she answer it?

Don't answer. Her heart rate increased with every ring.

He called three times, back to back. Halfway through the second time, Grayson switched on the radio and cranked up the music, not even caring what station it was on. Some kind of loud, thrashing heavy-metal band blared through the speakers. It soon reminded her of Josh, so she quickly changed it.

When the screen went dark on her phone, she let out a breath, blowing hair away from her face as she sank against the seat. Maybe his break was over, and he wouldn't call back.

Her phone buzzed once, the screen bursting to life again, and Grayson felt like she either wanted to cry or scream. She looked down at the text message: *Why aren't you answering your phone?*

If she replied, it would give her more time to get out of town. All she'd have to do is say she was in the bathroom when he called. He would buy it, although, she wouldn't put it past the psycho to have some kind of GPS tracking on her phone. Just the thought of him doing that almost made her jerk the wheel around and aim back home.

Stop it, she told herself, banging the steering wheel with both hands.

Flustered, she turned down the music, missing the knob twice before she finally made contact.

The phone rang again, and Grayson jumped with

a shriek.

Her mind stilled. She grabbed the phone, rolled down the window, and tossed it into the night.

"Fuck you, Josh!" she yelled, sticking her head partially out of the window. Grayson felt a calm wash over her as she sat back in her seat and laughed.

For the first time in three years, she felt like a huge weight had been lifted from her shoulders. She finally felt free to be herself, and it was fucking amazing.

She recognized the song that came on: one of her favorite Travis Tritt tunes. Josh hated country music, especially the songs she liked, so she turned it up louder.

Oh yeah, Grayson thought, *effing amazing.*

A few more miles passed until the reality of the situation started to creep into Grayson's head. Where in the world was she going to go? All she knew was she was on the highway and headed east. She didn't have much money and was in the middle of college, so she had no real skills. It hit her that she could go anywhere she wanted; she never felt so alive. She could get a job waitressing or work in a bookstore. All that mattered was that she was free.

As long as Josh doesn't find me, Grayson thought. She couldn't help it she was still scared of that poor excuse of a man. And that really pissed her off.

She knew he would look for her. What better reason to reinvent herself? She was twenty-one years old, and she was about to start a new life. The thought both terrified and excited her at the same time.

Maybe I should call Mom, she thought, glancing at the clock. It was only nine; she'd still be up, probably watching the news. She needed to tell her mother that she was okay, because Josh would call her when he couldn't find Grayson. He'd done it before, managing to scare the crap out of her mother.

Her mom lived in Tennessee, where she'd recently moved to be closer to her brother and his family. Ethan was a soldier, married with two kids. His wife, Heather, was sweet, but there was no denying her OCD tendencies. Grayson tried to remember the last time she'd seen any of them. It was well over a year since she had seen her brother's face.

Josh always insisted they spend the holidays with his family. A wave of sadness washed over her when she thought about her twin sister, Luna. They used to be inseparable, and now they barely even spoke, except for the occasional text messages.

My brother isn't a fan of Josh, either, Grayson thought, rolling her eyes. *Note to self: If your family hates your boyfriend, there is probably a good reason behind it.*

Grayson didn't want to return to her family for good. She needed her independence, but she could definitely visit. Take a break, maybe save up some money before she left for someplace better. Either way, she did need to call her mom before Josh did.

She reached for the cup holder—and realized she no longer had a phone.

"Oops," she said, and laughed again. The phone call would have to wait.

Grayson drove for hours until she felt like her eyes were going to cross. She passed a sign that read, *Albuquerque – 20 miles* and figured it'd be better to stop before she reached the city. A brightly lit exit loomed closer: gas stations, hotels, fast food, and a giant Wal-Mart. She took the off-ramp and pulled into a Days Inn.

As the engine cooled, Grayson leaned her head against the seat rest and stared into the empty lobby. It was the dead of night. Other than the clerk behind the desk, nobody else was in sight. She'd never stayed at a hotel on her own before. It looked a little seedy, but she was too tired to drive any farther.

A bell rang when she pushed through the door. The lobby was clean, at least, though the walls could use a new paint job and the coffee smelled days old. Grayson walked up to the counter, nose wrinkling as she took in the clerk's appearance.

He wore the typical staff uniform of a button-down and khakis, but had a huge beer gut that hung over his pants, completely concealing his belt. His hair was curly, and he had a bushy mustache with some kind of white stuff in it. He gave her a once over, his eyes staring too long at her breasts.

Creepy, she thought with a shudder. "I need a room."

"You all alone, sweetie?" His voice was too high-pitched for his body.

Never let a strange guy know you're by yourself. Her big brother taught her better than that. She thought fast and blurted out, "No, I'm here with my mom. She's waiting in the car."

"That's good." He glanced over her again, and Grayson fought the urge to cross her arms over her chest. "It's not safe out there for young women as pretty as you to be on their own."

Grayson slid her credit card across the counter, ignoring his leering eyes. "One room, two beds."

"You got it, pretty girl." The clerk reached for

the card before she could pull away, and his fingers brushed hers.

Yuck.

Key cards in hand, she was thankful to leave behind his beady eyes and made her way back out to the Jeep. She felt his gaze on her even as the Jeep pulled away from the curb.

Creepy.

She probably shouldn't have stopped so late, she thought, taking the parking lot around to the back of the building. If she weren't about to fall asleep at the wheel, she probably would have done otherwise. Tomorrow, she would have to be smarter: drive during the day, stop for dinner, maybe.

She needed to be safe inside before the sun went down, bottom line. That unfortunately meant not a whole lot of sleep would be happening tonight. She had been in such a rush to leave, she hadn't planned anything out. Grayson both needed and wanted to put as much distance between her and Josh as possible.

One-thirty-two was a corner room. Grayson shoved the door to overcome the resistance of thick carpet then clicked on the light and groaned. The room was tiny and musty with industrial-grade furnishings and a comforter so worn it looked as old as her grandmother. On the bright side, it didn't reek of cigarette smoke. Grayson dropped her bags on the single armchair by the window, then bolted the lock and slid the chain into place.

She sank into the bed, exhaustion hitting her even more now that the car was no longer buzzing beneath her. She looked down at herself. She'd spilled coffee on her T-shirt somewhere near the state line, and her jeans were dirty from getting in and out of the Jeep.

She realized she hadn't showered since early that morning.

She still smelled like Josh.

Oh, my God, EW.

Fifteen minutes later, scrubbed twice over and in clean pajamas, Grayson fell into bed. With a thin line of light peeking from the bathroom, and the room smelling of soap, she was fast asleep as soon as her head hit the pillow.

CHAPTER 4

Sunlight spilled through the crack in the curtains, and Grayson groaned, rolling over to cover her face. Her neck was stiff from the flat, shapeless pillow, and the musty covers across her cheek were rough. She definitely wasn't in her familiar bed.

Her eyes snapped opened, and everything came rushing back. She sat up, gripping the covers for support as she looked around the tiny, drab hotel room. She really did it. It wasn't a dream.

She was *free.*

No more Josh, no more being treated like crap—and absolutely no more tiptoeing around or pretending to be someone she wasn't. A slow smile spread across her face, and she flopped back to the pillow, profound relief trickling through her. She felt like screaming her excitement at the top of her lungs. Instead, she pressed both her hands to her face and smiled like a goofball.

After basking in the exhilaration for a few moments, Grayson sat back up and stretched.

Now what? What was that saying? *This is the first*

day of the rest of your life or something like that. Kind of corny, but it seemed to fit her situation just perfectly.

The first thing she had to do was contact her mom and sister. Surely, Josh had called them by now, as he always did anytime Grayson didn't answer her phone. But she'd been gone an entire night without contact, whereas before she'd always missed just one simple phone call. So her family was probably worried to death.

She pushed off the covers and jumped out of bed, practically skipping across the room to where her bag sat in the chair next to the door. She dug out her laptop and booted up the Mac.

Her heart stuttered when she saw all the messages from Josh on Facebook, Skype, and Messenger. He was completely flipping out, which didn't come as a surprise. Before she clicked off the programs, she glimpsed some of the messages, and her stomach turned.

Where the hell are you?
I'm going to find you, Grayson.
I told you it's not over until I say it is!
I'm sorry. I love you. Please come back.

That man was worse than a damn pinball machine; his emotions were all over the place. He'd say anything to appeal to her, to get her to come back, even after threatening and putting his hands on her.

Thankfully, he was no longer her problem.

Grayson's hands hovered over the keyboard as she debated on replying, but she really didn't want to engage in any more conversations with him. She had no patience to listen to him go between groveling and rage. A clean break was the only way to do this.

She pulled up her email account and found five emails from him. Ugh! She hit the delete button on all of them without opening them. New start, she reminded herself. A clean slate.

First order of business: reassure her mom that she was okay. She opened a new email and typed:

Mom,

I just wanted to let you know, I'm headed your way. I lost my phone, so I can't call. I need you to do me a favor. If you hear from Josh, just tell him that you haven't heard from me. We broke up... I'll explain when I get there. Thank you. I can't wait to see you all.

Love,
G

Then she pulled up Skype, shaking her head with a smile. Her twin sister, Luna, was going to throw a party when she heard the news. She'd hated Josh from day one. And Luna wasn't one not to tell you "I told you so" when she was right about something.

Grayson Alexander
I know you'll be doing the jig. I dumped Josh.
10/2/13 7:33 AM

Luna Alexander
No shit!? I'd hate to tell you I told you so, but...
10/2/13 7:34 AM

Grayson Alexander
I knew you'd say that! But yes, you win this time.

You called it. I left last night. I guess I'm going to Mom's. I don't know where else to go.
10/2/13 7:34 AM

Luna Alexander
Yes! I've been here for a couple of months. Double trouble!
10/2/13 7:35 AM

Luna is at Mom's? How had Grayson not known that? She was such a fool for not staying in touch with her family because of some jackass. She'd pulled away from them and her friends so much that she didn't even know what they were doing with their lives. She couldn't wait to be back with her family and away from his bullshit.

Grayson Alexander
You're at Mom's?
10/2/13 7:35 AM

Luna Alexander
Yeah, I came to visit Ethan and didn't want to leave. That and this place is crawling with hot guys. Who doesn't love a man in uniform?
10/2/13 7:36 AM

Grayson groaned. That was all she needed right now—her sister trying to fix her up.

Grayson Alexander
Why didn't you tell me you left Florida?
10/2/13 7:36 AM

Luna Alexander
Well, we haven't exactly kept in close contact since you left me for Josh...I mean Arizona.
10/2/13 7:37 AM

Grayson's shoulders slumped. What kind of twin neglected her other half for a man? She was suddenly filled with a different, altogether new type of self-loathing. Not only had she let herself be controlled by Joshua, but she walked away from her family. Not to mention her nearly ruined relationship with her best friend.

Never again, she thought.

Grayson Alexander
I'm sorry.
10/2/13 7:37 AM

Luna Alexander
You can make it up when you get here.
10/2/13 7:38 AM

Grayson Alexander
I'll be there in a couple of days. I told Mom I lost my phone, so if she asks that's the story, but we both know I threw that thing out the damn window. I'll probably stop and grab a prepaid, so I can check my messages. If you hear from Josh, you don't know where I am.
10/2/13 7:38 AM

Luna Alexander
If I hear from Josh, I'll tell him to go screw himself. Anyway, that asshole knows how I feel about him. I'm pretty sure I'd be the last person on earth he would call

to help him get you back.
10/2/13 7:39 AM

Grayson laughed and realized she really missed her crazy sister. That was so typical Luna—honest, blunt, and unknowingly, hysterically funny.

After she said good-bye and logged off of Skype, she didn't even stop to think. One by one, she deleted all her accounts and made new ones. New Facebook, new email, new Skype. Every single one she made private and blocked Josh. It was a pain, and took her nearly an hour to accomplish, but by the time she was done, she'd completely cut Josh from her life.

Well worth the time spent to get away from him.

Grayson closed the computer and wiggled her toes.

Freedom. The phrase made her think of her favorite movie, "Braveheart." Back when her Dad was still a part of her life, he introduced her to all of Mel Gibson's greatest hits. He could recite every single line from "Braveheart."

Yeah, but look where that "freedom" got William Wallace, she reminded herself.

He was killed for high treason. Hopefully, that wasn't a sign of Grayson's own fate.

No negative thoughts, she chided herself.

The first thing she was going to do was eat. She was starving. Well, the second thing. Shower first. Her hair smelled like mildewed sheets.

The water pressure was pathetic, so she didn't linger. She stayed in just long enough to wash off the feeling of sleeping under stinky motel covers. She slipped into a pair of jeans, a green T-shirt with the Recycle symbol, and flip-flops, and opted to go without make-up simply because she could.

After she was ready, she packed her things and stowed them in the Jeep, then checked out—happy to see the gross guy from the night before had been replaced by a pink-cheeked young girl who was fast and friendly.

The day was warm and bright as she walked into the parking lot, her stomach growling. She'd been in such a hurry to leave last night; she didn't bother to eat other than the apple and iced tea she'd grabbed at a gas station. She couldn't believe she was going to drive cross-country by herself.

Settling her sunglasses on her nose, Grayson made a beeline for the Waffle House next door.

The bell jingled as she entered the air-conditioned interior. The sound was abnormally loud and everyone turned to look, making her feel self-conscious. She was always the shy twin, leery of being the center of attention.

A chorus of a very enthusiastic *welcome and good morning* greetings rang out from behind the counter, and a rail-thin waitress smiled as she wiped down a table just inside.

"Seat yourself," she chirped.

Grayson grabbed a small table on the outside wall, so she'd have a view outside. She turned over the sticky laminated menu and glanced over the breakfast offerings, even though she already knew what she wanted.

The waitress came by with a mug and coffee pot.

"Coffee?" she asked.

Grayson smiled. "You read my mind."

"Coffee makes the world go round," the woman said and sat the pot down to pull out a pen and pad. "What can I get ya?"

Grayson ordered eggs, hash browns with cheese, bacon, and toast. She usually ate pretty healthy, so it was nice to order a greasy fattening meal. She'd lost over ten pounds since meeting Josh because he liked her to be on the slim side. She, on the other hand, preferred curves. Just another reminder of how bad he was for her.

Bring on the carbs.

Grayson felt awkward eating by herself. She realized she couldn't recall the last time she had been to a restaurant alone, and she didn't even have a phone to stare at so she didn't look pathetic.

Get used to it, she thought wryly. She needed to learn to be on her own, to enjoy her own company. Somewhere during the last three years, her personality was replaced with a submissive girl. She'd always been introverted, but she'd never been insecure before. Josh made her feel flawed, broken even. She shuddered at the thought. How could she waste three years of her life?

No more. Like a snake shedding its skin, Grayson was leaving that person behind.

For good.

CHAPTER 5

Two days later, Grayson crossed into Nashville city limits just as the sun was about to set. A beautiful orange glow blanketed the city. She followed the twists and turns of the road, marveling at the trees whose canopies were brilliant shades of copper, maroon, and yellow. It was a gorgeous display, something she hadn't seen in a long time. Seasonal changes were practically nonexistent in Arizona.

This is what fall is supposed to look like, she thought.

Though exhausted from the trip, she also felt warm and happy after two days on the road, alone with her thoughts and disconnected from anything hurtful or obnoxious. She didn't even miss her phone and its endless supply of social media...yet, anyway. She was sure, by the time she was standing still at her mom's house, she'd be dying for a distraction.

Only an hour more and she would be home. Well, to her mother's home, at least. She had no idea where her home was anymore.

She drummed her fingers on the steering wheel to the music. Her mom was off on a weekend scrapbook retreat, so she wouldn't be at the house. Grayson hadn't known events like scrapbook retreats even existed. Three whole days devoted to pasting pictures on thick cardboard and cutting shapes with curly-edged scissors, all in the name of preserving memories. Her mother would be in heaven.

At least Grayson would have privacy and time to get settled in while she figured out what she was going to do with herself. Maybe she could finish her degree online, or just take a year off and get a job. It would all get sorted somehow.

Not to mention she was way too tired to deal with the inevitable grilling from her family on exactly what happened back in Arizona. Right now, she just wanted to fall into bed and sleep for days.

Forty minutes later, she caught a glance of a Starbucks sign. Grayson flicked on the blinker and took the exit ramp. Why pass up a Starbucks? If Starbucks offered caffeine IV drips, she would be first in line; she lived for that place. Grayson was only about fifteen minutes from her mother's house, but her mom was a tea drinker. Her supply of instant coffee would do in a pinch, but who knew if the absent-minded woman even had milk?

Grayson decided to stretch her legs and go inside instead of hitting the drive-through. She rubbed her bare arms and quickened her step, her toes chilly in her flip-flops. It was just her luck a cold front had passed through that day, putting a bite to the wind that made for perfect coffee weather. For Tennessee, this probably wasn't all that cold, but she'd lived in hot, dusty Arizona for so long that anything below sixty felt arctic. She didn't think to grab a jacket or at least tennis shoes before leaving Josh's apartment.

All she had thought about was getting the hell out of there.

A wave of warmth and the aroma of coffee hit her as soon as she opened the door. Of course, there was a line of customers waiting. It wouldn't be a corporate-owned coffee house if that weren't the case. So she made her way to the restroom to freshen up and then took her place in line. Grayson found herself behind two women talking loudly about the dark-haired woman's asshole of a husband.

Nothing like spreading around your dirty laundry, Grayson thought, making a face. Grudgingly, she admitted how happy she was, knowing her fate was different than the dark-haired woman's. She wouldn't be standing in line at Starbucks complaining about being married to Josh.

She glanced around, desperate for something to take her mind off their asinine chatter. The cafe was crowded, full of college kids with books open on the table, couples chatting, and a few loners on computers. It was a great atmosphere, the kind of place she would have come to study back in Arizona.

Grayson noticed a guy sitting at a corner table, reading a book beneath a dangling lamp. The dim bulb cast his silhouette in a shadow, highlighting his strong jaw and broad shoulders. He glanced up, just an innocent flicker of his eyes, and their gazes locked.

Her stomach fluttered and her body temperature went up a few degrees. *What the hell?* Grayson was shocked at the immediacy of her reaction.

Quickly, she looked away and willed herself not to turn in his direction. He was just a random stranger in a café, nothing special. But she couldn't help herself; it was as if something was compelling her.

Trying to act nonchalant, she decided there was no harm in taking another peek. As if he felt her gaze, his head instantly popped up and he grinned.

Grayson stood frozen, her heart pounding. She couldn't even tell what color his eyes were at that distance, but she could tell he was sexy—that much was evident. The rugged, outdoorsy type of sexy, not the pretty-boy type like Josh. The guy exuded confidence and sex, stirring Grayson's desire. His sex appeal washed over her, heating her skin until her face was flushed. How could her body react so strongly to a stranger? She couldn't take her eyes off him.

It didn't help that he was staring back at her.

"What can I get you?"

Grayson turned, startled at the intrusion, and realized it was her turn to order. The short, blonde barista looked at her expectantly.

She fought the urge to fan herself, hoping her body temperature would ratchet down now that she wasn't caught in a staring contest with the sexy stranger in the corner.

"Um, I'll have a small caramel mocha."

"Ok, so a *tall* caramel mocha got it. Will there be anything else for you today?"

She shook her head no. She thought it was so annoying when the baristas corrected her after she said *small*. What the heck was the difference anyway, and wasn't the customer always right regardless?

"What's your name?"

"Grayson."

The curvy teenager wrote her name on the cup and handed it off to the girl working the bar. "Four-eighty is your total."

Grayson paid for her overpriced tall coffee, and

then made her way to the end of the counter, drawing closer to the hot guy with the book, making her heart rate increase again. She turned her back to him, sad that he didn't look up from reading this time.

She watched a sweet-faced barista effortlessly make her caramel mocha, all the while hyper-alert to *his* presence behind her. Why was she acting like an idiot? He was just a guy; he probably didn't even give her another thought after their brief yet oddly intense exchange of looks.

Once she got her drink, she made her way to the cream and sugar stand to grab a napkin and hightail it out of there. She turned to leave and slammed into a solid wall of muscle.

Shit.

Coffee spilled on her hand and down the front of his black T-shirt. She held the remains of her coffee out of harms way, too aware of how firmly her chest pressed against his. Horrified, she lifted her gaze.

He cupped her elbows with both hands and steadied her. His dazzling green eyes were ringed with gold and swept over her. He reached around her, grabbed a napkin, and wiped the hot coffee off her hand. She caught herself giving him the once over while his attention was elsewhere. He was hot with dark red hair framing rugged facial features.

"You all right?" he asked in a low voice.

Grayson mumbled something that didn't sound like English. Her breath caught as she took in his powerful frame. His stance was wide and his faded jeans clung to his muscular thighs. His T-shirt was stretched over his broad shoulders.

His smile softened his hard face. "Why don't you come and sit down with me?"

"Um, what?"

He tilted his head towards his seat. "The cafe is full. You can share my table."

Good grief.

All she did was make eye contact with the guy, and he thought that gave him the right to invite her to sit down? She'd clearly been in a relationship way too long, because she had no idea how to react to his question. Part of her was curious about a man who made her heart rate speed up with just a glance, but a much bigger part of her wanted to turn and run. She just got out of one relationship; she wasn't about to start another the moment she drove into town. Besides, she'd always heard two redheads were a disaster waiting to happen.

No thanks, she thought, *I have had enough disaster in my life for at least five more years.*

Although, her mother claimed she was only half redhead, the other half light blonde. So maybe it would only be half a disaster?

Snap out of it Grayson, she told herself, trying to get her shit together and not look like a blabbering idiot.

"I can't. I have to meet my family. But thanks for the offer." Grayson tried to step by him, but he shifted to block her.

"Can I at least give you my number?"

Oh my God, Grayson thought. This guy was persistent. He was hot as hell, but come on!

"Do you hit on every girl who walks through the door?" Grayson snapped. She wasn't going to let another man gain the upper hand on her so fast.

He laughed, his eyes crinkling at the corners, and she wondered how old he was. "Not all of them."

"Well, that's a relief. I guess I should feel special or something."

Someone behind Grayson cleared their throat, and she realized they were clogging up the condiments stand.

"Sorry," Grayson apologized, then brushed past the guy whose name she didn't even know, and hustled towards the door.

He didn't give up, however, and followed closely behind.

This guy can't take rejection. Or he's never experienced it. He was smoking hot after all, so it was a possibility.

Irritated as hell, she stopped and turned, "I told you—not interested."

His green-eyed gaze searched her face. Finally, he shrugged.

A shrug, really, that's all I get? This guy was making Grayson feel like she was bipolar.

"Grayson, just take my number. You can call or not, the ball is totally in your court. You can even throw it away as soon as you walk out the door. Just humor me."

Grayson's jaw dropped, but she shut it quickly. "How do you know my name?"

He tilted his head towards the cup in her hand, a mischievous smile upon his face. She felt beyond foolish. He probably heard the barista call out her name too. Josh made her into a completely paranoid human being.

"Wait one second," the stranger said, holding up a hand. "Don't leave yet."

She watched as he made his way to the front of the line, cutting in front of eight people, including the one in mid-order. He spoke to the cashier. He returned with a pen, gently extracted her cup from her hand, and in block letters wrote *DERRICK* and a phone number. His hands brushed hers as he handed the cup back, and it was as if a shot of electricity coursed through her body. Startled, she yanked her hand away.

What the hell kind of magnetic charge did this guy have? What in the world is happening to me?

Without another word, she turned and walked out of the cafe. She could feel his eyes on her as she crossed the lot and got into her Jeep.

In the comforting interior of her car, Grayson let out a deep breath and lifted her cup to eye the name and number.

Note to self: avoid Starbucks.

CHAPTER 6

A sigh of relief escaped Grayson when she turned into the quiet suburban neighborhood where her mother lived. The yards resembled tiny postage stamps: perfect green, landscaped squares with all manner of brilliant flowers and box hedges. Misty streetlights lined the sidewalks alongside pretty picket fences and discarded toys left by neighborhood children. It was similar to their old neighborhood back home in Florida. At least her mother's taste hadn't changed.

So much else had changed since the Grayson she graduated high school. She still found it hard to get used to the fact that her mom had moved to Tennessee. She had been positive her mom would retire and stay in Florida. Of course, it made sense that she would want to be closer to her only grandchildren, especially after her youngest kids had flown the coop. Grayson went to Arizona, and even though Luna remained in Florida, she moved into her own apartment not long after Grayson left.

She couldn't believe her sister was also in Tennessee. There was something to be said for the comfort of family and knowing one could always come home.

Case in point, Grayson thought as she pulled into the driveway at her mother's and cut the engine.

The house sat off to the left at the end of the cul-de-sac. Her mother had left the porch light on for her, and it brought a smile to her face. Her brother, a Green Beret, was extremely conscious about security. He'd spent his life drilling his sisters and mother on the importance of taking precautions: *Never let anyone know you're out of town, have your mail delivery stopped until you return, keep at least one light on in the house, set your alarm, et cetera...*

Hopping out of the Jeep, Grayson pushed her disheveled hair behind her ears and grabbed her coffee before getting the bags from the backseat. The security lights came on as she ambled up the driveway. Her shoulders ached from the drive, and her butt was numb for sitting down so long.

The flowerbed stopped her in her tracks, like it always did. Mom had always said a well-groomed garden could make any house feel like a home. Grayson thought back to her own crappy apartment in Arizona, devoid of flowers. Josh thought they were a waste of money. Anger welled up in her chest, but she was determined not to let her past influence her future.

She leaned down and smelled the yellow roses, a smile tugging at her lips. They were her mother's favorite. Their father used to bring her home yellow roses when he went away for work. *A promise of a new beginning,* he would say. Grayson's smile disappeared at that thought, and she rolled her eyes, readjusting her bag.

We see where that got Mom—alone.

Grayson found the small silver key beneath the empty flowerpot on the porch. Her brother would say it wasn't a safe place to keep it, but she had to get in somehow. She fumbled with the unfamiliar lock, and then pushed the door open. As soon as she entered the open foyer, she disarmed the security system using the same code as always. She shook her head at her mother's predictability. Ethan would not approve.

Her bags dropped with a thud onto the hardwood floors. She rubbed her face, feeling the exhaustion from the long drive. The faint smell of leftover sandalwood incense filled the air, and the bubble of the fish tank soothed her frayed nerves. Grayson rolled her shoulders and dropped her head, feeling the tension ease out of her.

The living room was dark, and the kitchen was bathed in moonlight, giving it an eerie glow. She brushed a hand over the wall just inside the door, searching for the switch. She flicked on the light. Colorful throw rugs were scattered atop shiny hardwood floors, and the walls were hung with houseplants and her mother's collection of eclectic tribal masks from Africa. A large, comfy-looking green couch dominated the living room, and next to it, toys were piled in a box.

Grayson looked at the clock. It was past nine. She'd assumed Luna would be here, but a quick check of all the bedrooms showed no bags or belongings to indicate Luna was staying here. Grayson considered calling her sister to let her know she'd made it home, but she was exhausted. The idea of staying up all hours of the night to catch up with her sister made her eyes feel heavier. She'd call her in the morning.

There was a note waiting for her on the table with

instructions on feeding the fish, watering the plants, and letting out the cats. She looked around and didn't see any cats. Maybe they were already outside. She shrugged and made her way to the spare bedroom down the hall, barely noticing the photos of her childhood that lined the hallway.

Grayson shed her clothes and crawled between the cool sheets. She was dead on her feet, but sleep wouldn't come. She twisted and turned, trying to get comfortable in the strange bed. What gives? She thought irritably. She should have been sleeping like a baby after driving for two days.

She wondered what Josh was doing, if he was going to come after her or let her go. She hated to admit it, but she was terrified he would track her down.

And do what? Make her leave with him? She needed to get a grip. She controlled her life, not him.

What about the guy from the coffee shop? Just the mere thought of him made her pulse quicken. It was crazy the way her body came alive from a look. She toyed with the idea of calling him, just because she could, but tossed out that idea almost instantly. She played their meeting over and over again in her head: his sure stance, his unusual eyes, and the electricity when he touched her.

No, she would definitely not call him.

She must have fallen asleep, because she was jerked awake late in the night by a loud thud. She bolted upright, her heart pounding as she listened intently.

What the hell was that?

Grayson grabbed the blankets, and her eyes darted around the room, her heart pounding. For a moment, all was silent, but then she heard another noise that sounded like something scraping across the floor in the kitchen. She bit back a shriek, and found herself wishing Josh was with her.

What the hell is wrong with me? Grayson gritted her teeth. She didn't need a man to make her feel safe. She tossed the blankets off and tiptoed across the room, looking for something she could use for a weapon.

Tension tightened her neck and shoulders. Grayson grabbed a big statue of Lakshmi, the Hindu goddess of prosperity and earth. Her mom would be pissed if she broke it, but it was the best she had in the situation. She was glad that Ethan had insisted they all take self-defense classes. She knew she could hold her own against most guys. It was just hard to remember that when fear coursed through her.

"Come on, Lakshmi. Don't fail me," Grayson muttered under her breath as she slid along the wall into the living room. The hairs on the back of her neck stood up. It was too quiet. Maybe she imagined the noise or dreamed it.

Her eyes adjusted slowly as she squinted to look into the kitchen, but she didn't see anything other than shadows dancing on the wall from the trees swaying outside—which was creepy enough. A shiver ran down her spine.

She was so focused on looking into the kitchen; she nearly had a heart attack when she felt something brush up against her leg.

"Holy shit!" she screeched, jumping backwards into the wall. Her gaze fell to the floor.

A fat white cat sat at her feet and purred, his heart-shaped face turned up towards Grayson.

"Where did you come from?" She leaned down and

picked up the fur ball. Her heart settled back into place. "You must have been hiding in Mom's room."

Relieved, Grayson turned on the kitchen light and glanced over the room. A cereal box she'd noticed on top of the fridge earlier in the night was now on its side on the linoleum, and tiny circlets of cereal were scattered across the floor. She laughed again, too elated to find there wasn't an intruder to care that she had a mess to clean up.

She did a walk through of the house to make sure there were no more surprises. Two more cats came out of the woodwork. How many cats did her mother have? Had she become the crazy cat lady at the end of the street?

Grayson returned to the kitchen and cleaned up the spilled cereal. She returned the box to the top of the fridge, then paused at the back window while the small white cat wove around her ankles. She could barely make out the lush greenery of the backyard. Tree limbs swayed beneath ethereal white moonlight. It looked peaceful and calm and worlds away from Arizona. When was the last time she had really felt safe? Certainly not since the first time Josh's temper flared.

She was sick of being scared all the time. She was stronger than that.

It's time to take my life back, Grayson thought firmly.

CHAPTER 7

The next morning, Grayson enjoyed a quiet breakfast alone with the cats. She checked in with her mom, who was in the middle of a class on using doilies in scrapbooking, and then she called her brother, Ethan, to set up a time to visit. She tried calling Luna but got her voicemail. After leaving her a message to let her know she was at Mom's house, Grayson lay down on the couch in front of the TV and stayed there all day.

The doorbell woke her up from a nap later that afternoon. Groggy, she rolled off the couch to answer it, the hardwood cool beneath her feet. She swung the door open and found the mirror image of her own face: long strawberry blonde hair, a sprinkle of freckles, clear blue eyes set in an oval face with full lips.

Grayson's twin pulled her into a crushing bear hug.

"I can't believe you finally dumped that jackass." Luna's voice was muffled in Grayson's hair.

Pulling back from the hug, Grayson grinned. "I figured you'd approve."

"Damn straight!" Luna shoved past her and kicked the door shut. "And now for the first time in your life, you are going to have some fun."

Grayson groaned. Her twin sister was her polar opposite. Luna was outgoing, outspoken, and always the life of the party. She rarely settled down with a guy for longer than three months, her reasoning being life was too short and there were too many men to experience.

Not slutty at all, Grayson thought with a laugh.

Grayson had always been slightly envious of her sister's carefree ways, but it just wasn't her style. They looked the same, but they were wired differently. Her mother claimed it was because Luna was left-handed and Grayson was right-handed. Just another one of her mother's quirky theories.

"I called you earlier. Where were you?"

"Work. Gotta pay the bills, you know." Luna looked around the living room. "Where's Mom?"

"Some scrapbooking retreat."

"Ah, I forgot about that. She's had it planned for ages. Well, that works in our favor," Luna said with her devilish smirk. "We don't have to explain why you won't be returning home tonight."

Grayson narrowed her eyes at her sister and frowned. "I'm not sure I like the sound of that."

"Grayson, have you looked around this town? It's a hot bed for sexy beasts. They are everywhere. This town is crawling with soldiers, and half of 'em are just passing through the base for training."

Grayson liked the sound of hot guys just passing through. If there was one thing she knew, it was that she wouldn't get into another long-term relationship. At least, not for a very long time. She needed to work on herself.

Luna breezed into the kitchen. She never missed anything, immediately honing in on Grayson's discarded Starbucks cup from the night before. Luna picked it up from the counter and spun it in her hands.

"Who's Derrick?"

Grayson's face flushed as the memory of last night's Starbucks meeting crossed her mind. The harder she tried to forget about the sexy stranger, the more she thought about him. It was annoying.

Luna smirked. "Only here a day and already got a number. I'm impressed little sister."

Grayson rolled her eyes. Luna loved to throw it in her face that she was the older twin. It had been ongoing all their lives, and it was ridiculous. "You're only two minutes and fifteen seconds older than me. Isn't it time we let the whole older-younger sister thing go?"

"Stop avoiding the question." Luna raised an eyebrow and stared down at the cup.

"Just some guy who gave me his number at Starbucks yesterday. He's no one." Grayson grabbed the cup from her sister's hand and tossed it into the garbage can under the counter.

"Was he hot? 'Cuz if you don't want him..." Luna headed for the trashcan.

Desperate to get her sister's attention off the phone number subject, Grayson spoke up loudly. "I was thinking about heating up a pizza. Are you hungry *older sister?*"

It was exactly the distraction that continuously served her well. Luna was always hungry.

"I'm starving," her twin responded, doing an about-face and heading towards the refrigerator.

Grayson waited until Luna had her face in the freezer, and then pulled off the sleeve of the cup and shoved it into her pocket. She had no idea what possessed her to do such a thing. It wasn't like she was ever going to call the guy. *Right?*

Luna turned, pizza box in hand, and eyed Grayson. "You need to put on some weight. I don't want to be known as the chubby twin."

Grayson rolled her eyes. "You're far from overweight, and you know it."

"Still. You're too skinny."

"Fine. I'll even have desert. Would that make you happy?"

"Very."

"Where are you staying? I thought you would be at Mom's house." Grayson leaned against the counter and watched her sister pull the pizza out of its box.

"I got a little studio apartment close by. You know me and Mom can't get along long enough to live together."

That was true. Luna drove their mother crazy. Their mother didn't agree with her lifestyle or choices, and Luna wasn't one to keep her opinion to herself. Grayson thought it was really because they were too much alike, but neither of them liked to hear that reality.

"It's weird," Grayson said. "The whole family's back together after going our separate ways."

Luna shrugged. "Not really. Ethan's always been the esteemed child, so it makes sense that Mom would follow him. I hated being in Florida, and you took off to the Wild West."

Grayson already missed Arizona. Her love of geology had been the driving force behind moving across the country. Once she realized how many science classes she would need, she'd changed her degree to counseling. Grayson left midway through her senior year to get away from Josh.

Panic rose in her chest as she wondered if she'd made a huge mistake. She should have at least gotten her degree before she split. Her decision to leave was rash and not carefully thought out at all. But she wouldn't be going back.

"Earth to Grayson," Luna said, waving her hands in front of Grayson's face.

Grayson snapped out of it and focused on her sister again. "What?"

"I said has Ethan come by?" Luna opened the oven and slid in the pizza.

"No, not yet. I'm supposed to go over for dinner tomorrow. I'm surprised I caught him home. It seems like he's always overseas these days."

"Yeah, he just got back, so he'll be around for a few months. I'll go with you. I haven't seen the little demon spawns in a while."

"Luna! Don't call them that!" Grayson laughed, because she knew it was true. Those kids were little terrors.

Luna shut the oven and turned around. "Okay, let's talk about what you're going to wear tonight." She looked down at Grayson's jeans and T-shirt with disdain.

"Forget it. I'll let you drag me to a bar, but you're not dressing me. We're not six-years-old anymore."

"You still dress like you're six-years-old. It's time to outgrow the tomboy look, Grayson. I'm surprised you're not wearing a baseball cap." Luna laughed. "Remember when you tried to convince everyone you

were a boy? I told you I would never let you live that down."

Grayson ignored her jab. When she was young, she hated all the attention they got as twins. Everyone called them pretty and fussed over them as if they were some kind of oddity. Grayson had thought if she were a boy, she wouldn't have to deal with so much attention. Her plan backfired and only brought her more unwanted attention.

"I'm not getting dressed up. That's your thing not mine." Grayson folded her arms across her chest. She drew the line at clothing.

Luna tapped her lip and sighed. "Alright. You know I enjoy the attention more than you anyway."

"Obviously," Grayson said as she walked over to the fridge. She pulled the lemonade out and poured them both a drink. It was tart and cold, just the way she liked it. The smell from the pizza cooking soon filled the room, and both of their stomachs rumbled at the same time. They broke into laughter. Just like old times.

Okay, so maybe having a twin isn't that bad.

"So what was the straw that broke the camel's back? Why did you finally leave that loser?"

Grayson looked down at the floor. She wasn't about to tell her sister the truth. She didn't need Luna to get arrested for assault. She shrugged. "It just wasn't working out anymore."

"Did he hurt you? Because I swear I will string him up by his testicles if he did."

Called it, Grayson thought, thankful that she didn't tell Luna the real story.

"No, it's nothing like that. I was just sick of his jealousy."

"Hmm. I'm just glad you left him. He changed you, and not in a good way."

Grayson could tell Luna wasn't buying her jealousy story but was glad she didn't harp on it.

"Well, it's behind me now. One of my stupid mistakes. Live and learn and all that shit." Grayson knew her sister had questions, but she didn't want to talk about Josh or her life back in Arizona. She changed the subject. "Where are we going tonight?"

"There's a bar near the hotels by the mall called The Trap. It's where the guys who are only in town for a short time hang out. Usually under two weeks in town. Great place to have a fling. Trust me." Luna gave one of her wicked grins.

"Well that's a lovely name, The Trap." It sounded rather ominous to Grayson, but she'd learned long ago that it was pointless to argue with her sister. Every time Luna had a bright idea, she dragged Grayson with her, willingly or kicking and screaming.

Grayson mulled the idea over in her head. Truth be told, she'd always wondered what it would be like to have a one-night stand. Hell, she'd never had sex with anyone other than Josh. Maybe it was time to broaden her horizons.

Slowly, she nodded. "Okay. I'm sure it will be fun. We haven't hung out in forever."

"Oh, it will be fun alright," Luna said while doing one of her famous happy *I got my way* dances.

Something told Grayson she would probably regret going, but what the hell?

They sat in the living room eating pizza and catching up for the rest of the afternoon. When Luna made her way to the bathroom, Grayson pulled out the coffee sleeve with Derrick's number on it. It was cutting into

her leg. She shoved it under the chair cushion.
Just in case.

CHAPTER 8

Luna pulled the car into a gravel parking lot behind a building that looked more like a log cabin than a bar. A neon sign above the door announced, "The Trap." The R flickered in and out of animation. Several people waited in line to get inside, and the music was so loud it could be heard from the car.

Pulling down the visor, Luna applied mascara and then offered it to Grayson, who just shook her head. Sighing, Luna tossed it back into her purse. "Remember, walk in like you own the damn place. Head up, shoulders back, and make eye contact."

Grayson rolled her eyes. Her sister was so dramatic. "This isn't a movie."

"Seriously, no one knows who you are," Luna said, fluffing her hair in the rearview mirror. "These people don't need to know you're a nerdy bookworm who wouldn't know a good time if it bit her in the ass."

Grayson glared at her, but Luna just smiled sweetly and went on, "Today is the first day of the rest of your life, little sister."

Grayson had to laugh. She'd thought the same

thing on the long drive from Arizona. She really did need to turn over a new leaf, which was why she'd agreed to this in the first place. Glancing back at the bar, Grayson took in a deep breath. Here she was, about to walk into a bar full of soldiers, and she might even take one home. Josh would have been pissed. The thought of making Josh pissed only fueled her fire, and gave her the confidence to let go and have fun.

"Ready?" Luna asked.

Grayson grinned slyly. "Let's go."

The night was cool and smelled like rain beneath a cloudy sky, but that didn't stop most people from coming out in their summer clothes. Grayson wasn't sure if the two girls in front of them in line were wearing dresses or handkerchiefs for all the coverage the shiny cloth gave them. She looked down at her own demure blue jeans and sweater. At least, her jeans were tight and the sweater form fitting, so she didn't look too frumpy. She certainly felt underdressed, though.

At the doorway, a burly security guard checked IDs. His dark eyes did a double take when they walked up, and he let out a wolf whistle. "Damn girl. I didn't know there were two of you."

Luna tossed her long red-gold hair over her shoulder and preened. "Tiny, this is my little sister, Grayson."

Tiny? Grayson thought, eyeing his over six-foot frame, all muscles and beef.

Tiny nodded, his bald head shining under the neon lights as he accepted Grayson's ID, giving it a passing glance. "I don't know if this town is big enough for both of you. You're going to give the guys a heart attack when you walk in there."

Luna flashed a wicked grin. "That's the plan."

Grayson was sure her cheeks were red as roses. How did Luna have enough confidence for the two of them while Grayson had none?

She must have taken on that characteristic in the womb.

Tiny handed their IDs back. "Have fun ladies."

"Oh, we will, Tiny." Luna laced her arm through Grayson's and pulled her inside, a little excited skip in her step.

They were immediately assaulted by the noise and the smell of cigarettes and alcohol. The Trap was just like any other old bar: dingy, smoky, packed with people and music blaring so loud Grayson couldn't hear herself think. A group of guys turned to stare at them. Grayson shifted her feet and looked down, her automatic response to attention.

Luna elbowed her in the side. "*No one* knows you."

The reminder hit home, and Grayson stood up straighter, willing the confidence to take over. She even found the courage to smile, though whether it was a nervous grin or a sexy one, there was no way to tell. Arms still linked, Luna led the way, squeezing through the crowd to the bar. A group of clean-shaven guys parted to make room for them, flashing smiles in their direction. A couple of girls with short skirts and low cut shirts glared daggers at them, but Luna just smiled and waved.

Behind the bar, a good-looking bartender with huge tattooed arms turned to face them. He had dark hair and pale green eyes. "Whoa. I'm seeing double here. I obviously need more sleep." He winked.

Grayson fought the urge to groan. A lifetime of twin jokes got old long ago.

"The usual, Luna? Times two?"

Great. Luna was on first name basis with the bouncer and the bartender. Had her sister turned into a lush while she was away? Scratch that. Had she turned into even more of a lush than she already was?

"We may look alike, but the similarity truly ends there." Luna tapped her fingers on the counter. "I'll take the usual, and she'll have a Jack and Coke."

The bartender nodded and pulled out a bottle of beer from the cooler beneath the counter, then slid it across to Luna. As the bartender mixed Grayson's drink, a broad-shouldered guy much older than they were threw money down.

"On me," he blurted out.

Luna turned and gave him one of her hundred-watt smiles. "Thank you, but buying our drinks doesn't mean you will be getting us into bed," she yelled over the music.

Grayson sucked in a breath, dropping her head low and willing herself to disappear. Her sister was so over the top. She always said the unexpected. For the tenth time since they'd pulled into the lot, Grayson felt her face get warm.

The man laughed. "Just watching the two of you is enough for me."

Luna tiptoed to kiss him on the cheek, and then led Grayson by the hand over to the only empty table. Within moments, a waitress came by, setting down more drinks. "The guy at the pool table sent them over."

Grayson turned to where she indicated. A tall, skinny guy tipped his cowboy hat with a smile, and then turned back to his game.

Luna tapped her fingernails on the neck of her new beer. "Another good thing about this place, I never pay to get in, and I never pay for a drink. They like the eye candy. This is a military town. The guy-to-girl ratio is ridiculous, I love it."

Grayson wasn't comfortable with the attention at all. She took a huge swig of her drink, and the liquid went down smoothly, loosening some of her muscles. She'd need a couple for liquid courage, but she'd have to watch her intake. It was a long time since she'd last gone out drinking. She knew her sister could drink her, and some grown men, under the table. The last thing Grayson needed was to get drunk and make a fool of herself.

Luna leaned upon her elbows across the table, her blue eyes sparkling. She motioned to the bar. "Pick one."

"Pick one?"

"Yeah, you can have any one of these guys. All you gotta do is decide which one you want. It's that easy."

Grayson looked at her sister like she'd lost her damn mind, but she did scan the bar. It was dimly lit and packed. Some people were out on the dance floor dancing to the local band playing, while a bunch crowded the bar, yelling to get the bartender's attention.

She honed in on a group of men gathered at the corner, all of them a bit more chill looking than the rest of the rowdy bar. There wasn't one woman near them, which was odd considering they were an attractive group. Grayson noticed a single guy standing off to the side of the group. He was obviously with them but hung back, one hand holding a beer bottle as his eyes scanned the bar.

Perfect, Grayson thought. He was tall and lean with short-cropped dark hair, the complete opposite of

Josh.

Grayson nodded towards his direction.

"That one."

She didn't really think it was as easy as picking a man out by appearance and guaranteeing to nab him. It was true that genetics had been good to Grayson and her sister, but there were a lot of pretty women at the bar. She felt like they were ten again and playing some silly game. She was humoring her sister because it was easier than ignoring her.

Luna nodded her approval. "Should have known, the leader of the pack."

"What does that mean?"

"Those guys are Marines. He's in charge; that's why he's standing back and watching."

"Marines? I thought this was an army town."

"Marines," Luna said matter-of-factly.

"What the hell would Marines be doing at an Army base?"

Luna laughed. "Training. All branches come here. I told you, hot bed for sexy beasts. Believe me now?"

"How do you know all this anyway?" Grayson asked, surprised that her sister had some kind of secret life she never knew about. She held up a hand. "On second thought, never mind. I don't think I want to know." She gazed at him thoughtfully. "He looks a lot older than me though."

Luna narrowed her eyes. "I'm sure he is. At least, mid-thirties, I'd guess. However, little sister, one tip I will share with you from my experiences: the older ones are much better in bed."

Excitement raced through Grayson's body. Could she do it? Have a little bit of fun for once? Let herself let go of her inhibitions? She could kill two birds with one stone: a one-night stand and sex with an older man. She wasn't as confident as Luna that she could just pick a man and have him take her to his hotel, but she figured it would be fun to try. Worst case, she went home alone. Not the end of the world. Plus, her liquid courage had ratcheted up a few notches while they talked, so why the hell not?

Grayson leaned to whisper in her sister's ear. "What about protection?"

Luna patted her purse, looking delighted as hell. "I got you covered."

Grayson's heart hammered at the thought. "Who did you pick?"

"Three guys over from yours."

Grayson counted and saw a guy who was much shorter with blond hair. He was laughing, his wide shoulders shaking and his head tossed back easily. She wondered what had made her sister pick him. She thought he looked way too much like Josh, and that was a total turn off.

Her eyes darted back to the dark-haired guy. He didn't seem to notice her. On the other hand, he didn't seem to notice anyone else either.

Luna stood up, and Grayson grabbed her arm. "Where are you going?"

"I'll be right back."

Grayson had to pick her jaw up off the table as she watched her sister walk over to the group of guys like she was some sort of celebrity. She leaned over and whispered something into the blond guy's ear. He turned and smiled, looking Luna up and down. Then she saw Luna point at her, and Grayson groaned. What was she thinking, following her crazy sister around? Hadn't she learned anything in twenty-one years? Her sister always got her into trouble.

Here we go again, Grayson shifted on the stool.

As Luna casually sauntered back to Grayson, the blond guy spoke to the one Grayson had chosen. The two men turned their attention over to her, and she wanted to sink into the floor. She was going to kill her sister.

Luna sat back down and smiled as the two men made their way over to the table.

Shit.

CHAPTER 9

Grayson's stomach flipped when the dark-haired man pulled up a stool beside her. She had no idea what her sister had said to the blond, who in turn had brought this sexy stranger to her side. Thankfully, the bar was dimly lit so he couldn't see how red her face was.

He leaned towards her resting his forearms on the table holding her gaze steadily. "What's your name?" Grayson froze; she didn't want to give her real name. She looked around for inspiration, and then glanced down at the amber and carnelian bracelet around her wrist. "Amber."

"Amber." He rolled the word around as if he was tasting it. "It's nice to meet you. I'm Todd."

Grayson raised the glass to her lips finishing her drink, and then pushed it to the side to pick up the next. She wasn't sure why she'd lied about her name, but it was too late now anyway. Maybe if she pretended like she was someone else, she could actually go through with this madness?

Luna seductively led the blond out onto the dance floor, leaving Grayson alone with a complete stranger.

Bitch.

"Are you from around here?" Grayson asked loudly.

He shook his head. "I'm from California. We're just here for training."

"Are you in the military?"

"Yeah, I'm a Marine."

So Luna was right. She usually was, as much as Grayson hated to admit it. "How long are you here for?"

"We're leaving tomorrow. We've been here a couple of weeks already." He took a swig from his beer. "This is my first night out, a celebration of sorts." He glanced over at his friends. "I have to make sure the guys don't get into trouble though."

He really could be perfect for what she had in mind. She would never see him again, and he didn't even know her real name. She stared at his profile. He was a good-looking man and well over six feet tall. She had always liked tall men. Compared to her five foot two frame, it was a stark contrast.

"Ah, baby-sitter of the group?" Grayson said sagely. "That's how I feel about my sister most of the time."

"Yeah, something like that." He leaned in closer.

"So tell me about yourself, Todd."

"What do you want to know?"

"What do you do for fun?"

Todd's face lit up. "I love to golf."

Oh, boy. Grayson took another drink and could feel the alcohol start to take on even more of an effect. Her body temperature always rose a few degrees when she drank. Suddenly, the room felt very hot and her head was tipsy. But it helped to drown out the golf jargon her newfound date was currently spewing. She nodded at the appropriate times as she finished her drink. Todd was really nice, and he was definitely hot, but golf was not an aphrodisiac.

Turning to the crowd to search for her sister, Grayson was shocked to see Luna full on making out with her guy on the dance floor. *That girl has no shame,* Grayson quickly turning back to Todd before her sister realized she was staring for too long.

A couple of songs, and a few long golf stories later, Luna came back to the table, holding hands with the unknown guy.

"We're out of here." She eyed Todd. "Hey, what's your name?"

"Todd."

"Todd, take care of my sister, okay?"

He looked at Grayson and back at Luna. "Sure."

Luna grabbed her purse and kissed Grayson on the cheek. "I'll call you in the morning."

As Grayson watched her twin walk out the door, she promised herself she was going to strangle that girl in the morning.

"Sorry about that," she spoke up, turning back to Todd.

He lifted a dark eyebrow. "Sorry about what?"

"Her. My sister, I mean." Grayson laughed. "I promise. We're nothing alike. This is her scene. She just dragged me along."

"No problem. I have to stay here until closing anyway. Remember, it's my job to make sure there's no trouble. Afterwards, I can drive you home."

"It's okay. Actually, I think I'll go." Grayson stood to leave, giving him a smile. "I can catch a cab home."

Todd reached for her, his calloused fingers brushing her bare arm. "Why don't you stay around a while? Keep me company. This isn't really my scene either."

Grayson studied him, looking for any bit of insincerity or humor, but he showed none. *Why not? It was stay with Todd or go back to her mom's empty house full of crazy cats.*

She sat back down.

They spent the next three hours talking about hobbies—thankfully, no more golf—as well as her sudden move back from Arizona. She kept all mention of Josh out of it. Todd seemed like a nice guy, and so far he hadn't made her uncomfortable at all.

The band called out *last song* and the bartender followed with *last call.* Grayson shared a smile with Todd. By now, she'd had a total of five drinks and was buzzed, so her grin was wobbly.

"Do you want to come and stay in my room? My hotel is right across the street. I promise I won't try anything." Todd paused. "You don't seem like you should be alone in a taxi, and I've had too much to drink to drive you home."

Bolstered by the alcohol, Grayson ran her eyes over his body and wondered if he was good in bed. It sent a thrill through her, desire uncoiling in her abdomen.

"Yeah. Taxis do kinda creep me out at night," she agreed. "That would be great."

They walked into the cool midnight air and through the parking lot to a hotel across the street. She felt exhilarated, high almost. He didn't try anything on the walk. No touching at all, not even a move to hold her hand. Grayson couldn't help but feel disappointed. She wondered if he really planned to be a perfect gentleman. If that were the case, she would have to make the first move. That would be another first she could check off her list if that ended up happening.

Todd fumbled with the key card as he slipped it

in the lock, and he let out a nervous laugh. Grayson thought it was cute. He was cute—even better looking in the light. She could have definitely picked much worse.

"I can give you a T-shirt to sleep in if you want," Todd said as they walked into the room. He actually went over to his suitcase to grab a shirt.

Was this guy for real?

Grayson figured if she was going to act like a different person and use an alter ego, she might as well go all out. While his back was turned, she yanked off her shirt and tossed it to the side, then shimmed off her jeans. She stood on the thin carpet in her underwear, shivering from the air conditioning.

Todd turned around, a white T-shirt in his hand. His eyes widened, and the shirt fluttered to the carpet. The room fell into silence. Nothing but the steady whir of the air conditioner was between them.

Grayson steadied herself with a single deep breath. Reaching back, she unhooked her bra and let it fall.

I kinda like my alter ego, Grayson couldn't help but think to herself. She felt free, like a confident woman. *Finally.*

CHAPTER 10

Grayson waited for his reaction, barely breathing.

For a moment, he seemed speechless. Then he moved his hands into a prayer position across his chest, looked at the ceiling, and whispered, "Thank you."

Immediately, Grayson laughed, her insecurity easing. Todd tore off his shirt, exposing washboard abs and a strong, shapely chest. He took a few steps forward, closing the distance.

Very nice, Grayson thought. She slid her hands up his warm chest as his lips crashed down on hers.

There was nothing sweet about the kiss. It was raw and carnal from the moment their lips met. Grayson clung to Todd's neck, desperate to feel the weight of his body on hers. She opened her mouth to him, feeling giddy with desire as his tongue slid against hers with a kind of sensuality Josh had never had.

She felt reckless and so unlike herself. She fumbled at the buttons on Todd's cargo pants, her fingers moving over him. He was already hard, which really turned her on.

She gripped the sides of his pants and tugged, exposing every glorious inch hidden beneath. There was no backing out now. Grayson dropped onto her knees and took the full length of him in her mouth. His skin was velvety soft, the head of him salty as her tongue moved around his shaft.

He moaned. "Oh, my God."

Grayson worked his cock, listening to the sounds of pleasure from Todd, and felt like a sex goddess. When she finally released him with an audible sucking sound, she stood up and their lips met again. He walked her back to the bed, taking her gently by the waist to push her down onto the comforter.

Kneeling between her legs, he held her gaze as he eased her panties off, then his warm lips trailed kisses down her stomach. His tongue dipped into the hollow between her legs causing her to arch her back and let out a moan. She grabbed as much of his hair that she could in an act of pure pleasure, tugging at it, showing him with her body how good he was making her feel. She was so wet she thought she was going to scream. She had to bite her lip to hold in a loud moan. His hands traced her body from her neck down, stopping to tease her nipples as she gasped, and then continued down her belly until she was squirming and mentally begging for him to enter her.

He pulled away and rummaged through his suitcase, emerging with a condom. Thank God. She had totally flaked and would have had unprotected sex. That sobered her momentarily, but it didn't last long. His lips and warm breath on the inside of her ankle made her mind go blank. Slowly, he made his way up her thighs.

"Please." She begged and lifted her hips.

"Patience," Todd murmured, crawling up to kiss her firmly, his cock resting against her for a brief, searing moment that made her mindless. "I'm going to enjoy every inch of you."

Her head felt like it was spinning out of control. She had never wanted anyone so badly in her life. Maybe, there was something to the no-attachment lifestyle her sister lived. His tongue flicked her clit, and she grasped his hair again and moaned. There was no use biting her lip this time, this man had skills. Josh had never been into oral sex, nor was he very good at it. But Todd was amazing at it. His tongue dipped into her, circling her nub, and he sucked until he brought her to climax, making her entire body shudder.

Then, he roughly turned her over, his weight pressing her breasts into the bed. His large hands grasped her waist, and she wiggled her ass, needing to feel him inside of her.

She could have cried when he finally entered her, every hard inch of him opening her and filling her. Her body was flushed with pure sensation. His hips pumped, their bodies moving together as she lifted her ass and rocked back on him, losing herself in the pleasure.

Hours later, their bodies slick with sweat and the mattress half on the floor, Grayson collapsed onto the bed, trying to catch her breath. She hadn't known sex could be that good.

Todd lay back, unworried by his nudity as he clasped his hands behind his head. He smiled. "You are incredible."

"I've never done this before..." Suddenly shy, Grayson pulled the sheet over her chest.

"What, a one-night stand?" Todd turned on his side

to stare at her. For the first time, she realized his eyes were blue. Dear God, she'd just had sex with a man and she didn't even know his eye color or last name.

She nodded.

"Well, I'm honored." He ran a hand down the side of her face. The move felt too intimate for her comfort, which was absurd since they'd just spent hours in positions she didn't even know existed.

"I wish I had met you the day we got here. I would have had you waiting for me every day after work. You've seriously just made this one of the best nights of my life."

"I'm sure that's an exaggeration." Grayson flipped onto her back and stared at the ceiling. "Either that or you've lived a very dull life."

"It's really not an exaggeration at all. Best surprise I've had in ages."

"I didn't know it would be so...good."

Todd laughed. "I gave it my best. You know, we come back here once a year, and also go to Memphis twice a year. It's not that far of a drive."

Grayson chewed the inside of her lip. He must have sensed her hesitation.

"Let's rest awhile and see about a repeat performance. I'm going to jump in the shower."

Grayson nodded and flopped her head to the side as the bathroom door shut behind him. What the hell had she just done? She'd had sex with a complete stranger!

I must be out of my mind.

She heard the water turn on and reluctantly jumped up. She found her jeans and sweater, and located her underwear half under the mattress, but she couldn't find her bra. She didn't know how long he

would be in the shower, so she decided to go without it. Quietly, she stepped into her shoes, and then she slipped out the door.

She wondered what Todd would think when he got out of the shower, but she didn't want this to go any further. She didn't want a morning after walk of shame, or a promise of a future meeting. It was going to stay exactly what it was: a one-night stand.

CHAPTER 11

Luna burst through the front door without bothering to knock. She was wearing the same clothes she'd had on last night, and her usually immaculate hair was disheveled. Luna was wild, but she was usually more put-together than this. She tossed her purse to the floor just inside and slammed the door.

Grayson noticed the dark circles under her sister's eyes and raised an eyebrow. "Long night?"

"I can't believe you left me without a ride home." Luna flopped on the couch, her long legs stretching to the coffee table. She sank against the cushions and closed her eyes.

Grayson gaped at her. "Seriously? You can't believe *I left you?* That's rich." Grayson set Pepper, the fluffy black-and-white cat, on the floor and glared at her sister. "You left me alone at a bar with a random guy. You knew I'd been drinking. What was I supposed to do? Come back and wait for you to stumble through the parking lot sometime before dawn?"

Luna flipped a long, messy braid over her shoulder and shrugged. "I knew it was the only way to get you to do something reckless for once."

Grayson had been sitting quietly in the living room petting the cats for the last thirty minutes, her mind slowly mulling over how different her life was now. Her sister's wrinkled, day-old jeans drove that idea home. Alarmed, Grayson realized she hadn't heard a car drive up. "How did you get here?"

"I walked. Details. Now."

Heat rose in Grayson's cheeks, and she avoided her sister's probing gaze. She may have had sex with a random stranger, but that didn't mean she felt comfortable talking about it.

"OH MY GOD! You really did it?" Luna squealed, leaning over to punch Grayson in the arm.

"Yes. Are you happy?" Grayson rubbed the tender spot on her bicep, thinking Luna's knuckles were like razor blades. "I've officially crossed over to the dark side. I had my first one night-stand."

Luna turned onto her side, her legs beneath her and her face pressed against the back of the couch as she smiled at Grayson. "And?"

Grayson didn't bother to fight her grin. "I loved it."

"*First* one-night stand." Luna smirked, waggling her eyebrows suggestively. "I like the sound of that. Here's to many more. So how was he? Good? I need details woman."

Without waiting for a reply, Luna leapt to her feet and left the room.

Grayson rolled her eyes and followed her sister, too used to her sister's Ping-Pong table style thinking to be anything more than amused. She dropped into a kitchen chair as Luna turned on the kettle. "He was amazing. Well, in bed. He was boring as hell until the clothes came off."

"I knew it!" Luna laughed, opening the cabinet where their mother kept the tea. "My guy was okay, nothing to write home about." She tossed a box on the counter and turned to the mugs. "Kinda on the small side, if you know what I mean, though he did have some serious stamina."

Covering her ears, Grayson laughed. "That's enough. Let's keep our torrid sex details to ourselves."

"You want tea or coffee?"

"Stupid question," Grayson responded dryly. "I know I was gone a while, but you know me better than that."

Luna chuckled, locating the jar of instant coffee in the spice cabinet. They were silent for a moment, the cooling fan in the fridge clicking on in the still kitchen.

"You wanna do it again tonight?" Luna asked, shooting a questioning glance over her shoulder as she measured out the instant coffee into a mug. "I know another great place for picking up guys. It's a totally different scene. Slower."

Grayson's heart pounded. Did she want to do it again? The excitement of doing something crazy, coupled with a night of pleasure was well worth the effort. But to do it again the next night? Maybe that was what Luna was used to, but Grayson wasn't sure she could do it. She'd definitely feel like a slut.

Luna turned around, leaning a hip on the counter. "Hello? Earth to Grayson?"

Just then, the sound of the front door opening echoed through the house. Grayson and Luna exchanged surprised glances, and as one, flew through the kitchen door and into the living room. Grayson was secretly grateful for the interruption.

Their mother practically floated through the door,

dropping a box to the ground with a thud. Pictures spilled out, followed by edging scissors and several containers of glitter. Her curly copper hair was as wild as ever. She looked like the retired hippy that she was in her long floral skirt, peasant top, and large hoop earrings.

"Hey, girls! What a sight for sore eyes. I've missed seeing the two of you together." She held open her arms, and Grayson obliged by running right into them.

Mom's smell was familiar: floral and powdery with a strong overtone of some kind of earthy incense. Grayson squeezed her mom's thin shoulders. "Thanks for letting me come here."

Mom swatted her away. "My children are always welcome. You know that." She took off her sweater and tossed it over the back of the couch. "So you finally came to your senses? It took longer than I expected."

Grayson shook her head. "It took way too long."

"I told you that your signs didn't belong together," Mom reminded her. "Maybe someday you'll listen to me. You're not going to be happy until you find a Taurus."

Their mother was an astrology guru. The first thing she'd done when they were born was have their charts made and their life plans set out before them. Of course like most children, they didn't listen to their parents. Maybe that could be Grayson's new pick up line: *Hey, baby, what's your sign?* Then she could only say yes to the Taurus men.

The three of them went into the kitchen to pour tea and coffee, leaving Mom's scrapbooking mess all over the entry foyer. Grayson and Luna spent the next twenty minutes listening to their mother gossip about the other scrapbook ladies. Apparently, a few of the ladies hit the bottle too hard, and one had a male visitor that was not her husband. Who knew scrapbooking could be so scandalous?

CHAPTER 12

Grayson pressed the doorbell of her brother's house. Within seconds, the door flew open. Her nephew, Matthew, leapt out at them, wearing a grotesque Halloween mask. He'd done the same thing since he was five. He was now *nine*. Needless to say, the novelty had worn off, but Grayson and Luna humored him by jumping back with surprised shrieks.

"Let them in," Ethan yelled from somewhere in the back of the house.

Matthew groaned and threw off the mask. "Come in."

"What, no hugs? You haven't seen me in ages." Grayson put her hands on her hips and glared at the little boy who was not so little anymore.

"Gross. I'm not hugging you." He took off and ran up the stairs.

"You really know how to make a girl feel loved," Luna yelled up after him.

Ethan appeared in the hallway. "My two favorite sisters," he said, yanking them both into a hug. He looked great. His dark hair was starting to grey a little at the temples. His grey eyes and strong jaw made him very appealing to the ladies. Ethan was virtually a spitting image of their father, while the girls took more after their mom. Ethan's similarities to their father almost always made Grayson think of him. Now that he was no longer a part of their lives, it wasn't a thought she was too fond of.

Grayson pushed the memories aside. They pissed her off too much.

Ethan was a few years older than she was, so they weren't that close growing up, but it sure was nice to relax in the arms of her oldest sibling.

"Where's Heather?" Mom asked, glancing around the open foyer.

"She had to run to the store to get something for dessert. She made a cake, and it was a little on the flat side, so she tossed it." Ethan rolled his eyes. Heather strived for perfection, and it sometimes got out of control.

Grayson wasn't sure how her brother's wife managed to keep the house immaculate with her two tornado children. The second tornado, Sarah, came running in from the back door, her brown curls bouncing around her perfect round face. She jumped into Grayson's arms.

Grayson buried her face in the girl's shiny hair, awed at how big she'd gotten.

"Aunt Grayson!" Sarah said happily, her feet bouncing. "I missed you."

Grayson felt a wave of anger at how long she'd stayed away. She didn't know whether to blame herself or Josh. Both, maybe.

"Come on out back," Ethan continued, motioning for them to follow him. "I invited some of the guys from my team over for a cookout. Everyone's outside. Carry your shoes so you don't give Heather a heart attack."

Grayson put Sarah back on the floor, and she zipped away again. Grayson slipped off her shoes, leaving them beside her sister's platform wedges and her mother's Birkenstocks. The three of them followed Ethan across the plush beige carpet of the living room, and into a large open kitchen full of stainless steel appliances and pristine marble counters, then finally out the back door.

The backyard was like a mini-paradise. Large, leafy ferns surrounded the cobblestone patio, and pale solar lights lining a gurgling pond were just starting to glow in the evening light. A large table sat under an umbrella covered in cartoon palm trees. A group of men gathered just beyond the edge of the patio, sipping cans of beer in shorts and T-shirts.

Grayson nearly tripped when she made eye contact with a very familiar man.

Holy shit, she thought, frozen in place for a split second. *The guy from Starbucks. Derrick. What the hell is he doing here?*

She glanced away and hoped she didn't look as shocked as she felt. She hated that he could get her pulse racing by his presence alone. *This cannot be happening.*

"Hey, guys. These ladies here are my mom and my twin sisters." Ethan tilted his head towards them.

"Damn, Ethan. You've been holding out on us." A huge guy with mocha skin stood in front of the smoking grill with a grin.

"Marcus, don't get any bright ideas. My sisters are off-limits to you bozos."

Luna put her hand on her hip and smiled. "I think

we're old enough to make our own choices. I, for one, happen to love bozos."

Marcus laughed. "I like it. She's got spunk."

Ethan went around the group of six guys and introduced them all, but Grayson was too shocked at seeing Derrick that she barely mumbled in reply. Luna, on the other hand, was already in her element, flirting with everyone.

Grayson was happy to stand in the background and let her sister shine with all the attention, as usual. It definitely made her life easier, having an outgoing sister.

She stole another glance at Derrick. What were the chances? One in a million? And why the hell was her stomach down to her toes like some silly high school kid? She wanted to bolt, but she had no logical reason to leave.

Instead, she willed herself to not look in his direction, but it was useless. She was disturbingly aware of his presence. For the next forty minutes, every time she looked up, he caught her eye. He kept his face smooth and impassive, which was annoying. He could have shown some hint of recognition.

In a lull in the conversation, Luna glanced at Grayson, one shapely eyebrow arching. She waved at the group. "We'll be right back. Marcus, make sure my steak is well done." Luna took Grayson by the arm and dragged her into the kitchen.

The moment the door shut behind them, she shook her head. "No."

"No what?" Grayson said innocently, though she knew what her sister meant. It was like Luna could read her mind, which was annoying.

"Don't even think of it," Luna said firmly. "Those

guys are really off limits."

Grayson frowned. "What are you talking about? I didn't do anything. You're the one out there flirting, not me."

"You can't keep your eyes off old rusty out there. What's his name?"

"Derrick," Grayson answered, a little too quickly.

A glint of recognition showed up in her twin's blue eyes. "Derrick. As in coffee shop Derrick?"

"Yep. The same one." Grayson leaned away, glancing out the window. Derrick was laughing, his head tossed back and the last vestiges of sunlight glinting off his hair. God, he was sexy.

"Interesting." Luna tapped her manicured finger to her lip. "But, off limits. You do not want to get involved with a guy from around here. And you definitely don't want to get involved with a guy from Ethan's team. Special Forces guys are total dogs."

"What was that?" Heather walked through the door with bags in her arms. She was a lovely woman with a round, pretty face capped by curly brown hair. "Did I just hear you put down your brother and my wonderful husband?"

"Of course not." Luna straightened. "I was just telling Grayson she didn't need to get involved with anyone on Ethan's team."

"Which one?" Heather giggled, sliding her grocery bags on the counter. "I know all their dirty little secrets."

"Derrick." Luna said with disdain. "I mean I'll admit it he does have that sexy redhead thing going for him, but still. Grayson is newly single."

"I hate to say it," Heather said wryly, "but I agree with Luna on this one."

Grayson crossed her arms over her chest. "I never even said I liked the guy."

"Uh huh. Then why do you keep staring at him all googly-eyed?" Luna asked, crossing her arms to mimic Grayson.

Grayson rolled her eyes. "I do not."

"Seriously, he's not good for you." Heather started taking out the contents of the bags as she spoke. "Every team party he brings a different girl. I don't think he's ever settled down."

"I told you they are all dogs." Luna smirked. "I'm right once again."

Grayson was surprised to feel a bit of disappointment at the news. But she knew they were right. The last thing she needed was to start a relationship with someone, let alone a friend of her brother's with a reputation for being a playboy. That would be weird in more ways than one.

Mom came through the door. Her crazy curly hair looked alight like fire with the sun behind her. "There is way too much testosterone out there for me. Need any help in here?"

Heather smiled warmly. "That would be great!"

Grayson and Luna used that as their cue to escape back outside.

Grayson spent the rest of the evening avoiding Derrick. She had succeeded, until she came out of the bathroom after dinner. She wasn't paying attention and nearly slammed into him.

He grabbed her to steady her. His hand on her arm caused her breath to catch in her throat. Her skin warmed beneath his touch. Instantly, she was annoyed. Why did he have such an effect on her? Heather's warning echoed in her head.

His stance was casual, but there was nothing casual about his smile. It was intimate, sensual and seductive. Jesus, he barely touched her and she felt as if an electrical charge had passed between them. The sexual tension was palpable.

"Small world," he said, dropping his hand after lingering longer than necessary.

She was bewildered by this man and the sense of loss she felt when he removed his hand. "Very."

"You never called." He was standing so close, his warm breath on her face, his scent intoxicating.

She stepped back, needing to get away from him to get some air. She felt completely unbalanced around him. It was disturbing.

In the back of her mind, she was appalled at her thoughts. She wanted to know what his lips would feel like on hers. A mental image of his hands on her bare skin, caressing her neck and moving slowly down to her breast flashed through her mind. Somehow she managed to speak.

"You heard my brother. I'm off limits."

He gave her a crooked grin and his intense eyes bore into hers, causing her pulse to race. "I seldom follow rules."

"So I hear." Her heart thumped loudly in her ears.

Eyebrow raised, Derrick remarked, "Oh really? And just what have you heard exactly?"

"Just that you're quite the ladies' man, and I should steer clear of your womanizing ways."

"Interesting. Well then, I won't keep you." He brushed past her and went into the bathroom, the door shutting smartly behind him.

Grayson cringed. Well, that wasn't what she expected. Grayson released a shaky breath. She was surprisingly irritated that he hadn't tried harder.

Oh well, if he was going to give up that easily, he probably wasn't worth her time or energy.

CHAPTER 13

Grayson made it through an uneventful week functioning on automatic. She'd put in a few job applications around town, but so far she hadn't heard anything back. Her mother insisted she didn't need to help with the bills, but Grayson felt like she was mooching off of her mom. She was too proud and loved her mother too much to use her like that. Hopefully, something would turn up soon so she could feel more independent again.

It'd been a week since her one-night stand, and Grayson was still surprised she'd gone through with it. She sat on the couch, surfing through the channels. She congratulated herself on escaping another night out on the town with her crazy sister, until just before nine. The door burst open, and Luna sashayed into the house.

With her hand on her hip in her usual dramatic flare, she glared at Grayson. "You're not even ready?"

"Excuse me? What exactly should I be ready for?" Grayson sighed and clicked off the TV, setting the remote control on the end table.

"Seriously, do I always have to spell everything out for you?" At Grayson's blank stare, Luna crossed her arms and huffed. "It's Thursday night...ladies' night."

"And your point Luna? I know we're twins, but we both know that the twins can read each other's minds concept is bull."

"My point, little sister, is that you need to get your ass up and get dressed. You can't lounge around in your pajamas all the time. You're starting to make me depressed."

"I don't feel like going out," Grayson argued. "Let's just stay in and watch a movie. We can pig out on popcorn, just like old times."

Luna rolled her eyes and shook her head in disgust. "Seriously, how can you look so much like me and yet be so lame?"

Narrowing her eyes, Grayson snapped, "Thanks."

Mom walked in from the kitchen, drying her hands with a towel. Even in her fifties, their mother still had an impish beauty about her and seemed to be eternally young. "You know I hate to agree with Luna," she remarked, ignoring the face Luna made, "but I think she's right. You need to get out, Grayson. All of your moping is bringing me down, too."

Grayson's head twisted towards her mother. "Great, now I have both of you teaming up on me?"

"You're only young once, Grayson. Learn to enjoy it before it passes you by and you're my age." Mom tossed the towel at Grayson, who failed to catch it before it hit her cheek.

"Ok, fine." Grayson sighed. They were probably right. She wasn't moving on and starting a new life if she was sitting on the couch all day, watching nonsense on TV. It was time she got back out there, no matter how much she really didn't want to.

Damn it.

"Yes!" Luna grinned from ear to ear. "Thanks, Mom."

"I didn't do it for your entertainment, love." She winked at Luna. "If you guys need a ride home, call me. I don't want any DUIs or accidents, and I especially don't want to get a collect call from jail."

"We'll take a cab if we need to," Luna agreed. "But don't wait up Mom. Grayson is going to stay at my place tonight."

"I am doing what?" Grayson had only been to her sister's little studio once. There wasn't exactly room for her to sleep over, which meant she would probably be sharing her sister's futon. Just like when they were little and shared a room. The idea almost sounded fun. *Almost.*

Luna held out her hand. "Come on, get your ass up."

One of these days, Grayson would firmly say no and deal with the fallout later. Unfortunately, today was not that day. She took her sister's offered hand and let Luna pull her off the couch.

"Get dressed." Luna pushed Grayson a few steps forward.

"I need to shower." Grayson trudged down the hallway to her mom's spare room where her clothes were stashed away. She pulled out a pair of jeans and an off-white long john shirt. It was snug fit, well worn and one of her favorites. Luna would disapprove, but she'd get over it. In record time, Grayson was showered, dressed and ready to go.

She was taking one last look in the mirror when the phone rang. Her mom had a habit of ignoring it, so Grayson grabbed it off the cradle without much thought.

"Hello?"

"Grayson?" Josh's deep voice came across the line.

She nearly dropped the phone. "Josh," she stammered, her heart nearly leaping from her chest.

"What the hell? Why did you leave like that? I've been going crazy looking for you. I even called the cops."

His heavy breathing crossed the line, making her stomach roll. She gripped the phone tighter, so irritated that her palms got all sweaty.

"Grayson?" Luna appeared at the doorway, face questioning.

Josh went on. "You could have at least replied to one of my messages, so I knew you were still alive."

Grayson turned around so her sister couldn't see her face. "I'm fine, Josh. I just had to get out of there."

There was a short pause, and then he said, "I'm coming for you."

The hairs on the back of her neck stood up. "Don't waste your time. We're over, I'm not coming back."

"Please, Grayson. I just want to see you." His voice cracked. "I'm spiraling without you. You were the only thing that held me together."

It was the crack in his voice that pissed her off the most. He could play the role of an apologetic boyfriend perfectly, down to drawing up tears.

"Sorry, Josh," Grayson snapped. "I can't be your crutch anymore." She slammed the phone down and took a deep breath, trying to compose herself before turning to her sister.

Luna opened her mouth to speak, but the phone started ringing again.

"Don't answer it!" Grayson yelled down the hall.

"I'm surprised it took him so long to find you," Luna said softly.

Grayson took a deep breath, realizing her fists were clenched, and slowly peeled her fingernails away from her skin. "Mom said he's been calling. I totally flaked. I shouldn't have answered the phone. Now he knows I'm here."

"Let's just get out of here." Luna turned and led the way.

They hurried out to Luna's car, a little two-door sports coupe in cherry red. Grayson settled into the passenger seat, and slammed her head into the headrest a couple of times. She was so annoyed with herself.

"Are you that worried about Josh?" Luna asked, concerned.

Grayson shrugged. "I doubt he'll really come here." But, inside, she really was freaked out about it. She knew he would cross the country if he thought he could get her back. Grayson was seriously considering making a move to another state. She'd only planned on coming to Tennessee temporarily anyway.

As Luna turned the key in the ignition, Grayson spoke. "We could always move somewhere together. We could go anywhere. You always said you wanted to go to New York City."

Luna turned and stared at her for a long moment, her blue eyes clouded with concern. "Grayson, you're scared of him. I don't need twin telepathy to know that."

She started to deny it, but knew it was useless. Her twin knew her better than she knew herself. "Yeah, a little I guess. He's just really possessive and jealous."

Luna didn't back out of the driveway. Instead, she appraised her for a long moment. "You're not telling me everything. I've never seen you scared of someone before, so I know there's a reason behind it."

Grayson didn't respond. She didn't want to admit to Luna exactly what life had been like in Arizona. She didn't want to admit she'd been so weak.

"We could always tell Ethan and let him take care of it," Luna said seriously.

"I don't want to drag Ethan into my pathetic love life."

"You know that's not what I meant."

Grayson tugged on a strand of her sister's hair. "If he shows up, I'll call Ethan. Okay?"

Luna nodded and leaned over to give her a half-hug. "You need a drink."

"Or three," Grayson agreed. Today was not turning out quite like she expected.

"Where are we going?" Grayson asked as they hit the road.

"There's a pub downtown. You'll love it. It's small, they make the best drinks, and of course there will be hot guys."

As Luna rambled, Grayson tried to get into the mood, but it didn't quite happen. She wanted to turn around and go home where she could try to piece together what to do next. Just hearing Josh's voice was enough to send her over the edge. Why couldn't he just let her go? She would be so embarrassed if he came to her mother's and made a scene.

Plus, the way her hands shook proved she was more scared of him than she dared to admit.

Tonight just wasn't going to happen, Grayson told herself. She wasn't quite up to another one-night stand so soon after the last one. She'd sit this one out and watch her sister have fun. That would be enough for her.

CHAPTER 14

Just as Luna had promised, the bar was small. Grayson liked it immediately. A single pool table took up a back corner, surrounded by a group of quiet guys gripping beer bottles and whiskey glasses. A wrap-around bar was hidden in the corner, flanked by dozens of tall round tables and stools. There was no dance floor, and a jukebox played a loud Nine Inch Nails song and flashed neon lights.

There weren't nearly as many people here as the first bar where she'd met Todd. It was a mixture of guys and girls, and no one seemed to pay Grayson or Luna much attention, which was refreshing. To say being with her twin usually made it hard to blend in was an understatement.

Grayson followed close behind her sister, who propped her elbows on the bar and flashed the bartender her winning smile as she ordered for the both of them.

"Don't worry—it will pick up soon," Luna said, offering Grayson her glass. "I wanted to get here early so we can watch them arrive."

Grayson accepted the drink with a surreptitious eye roll. Her sister was such a drama queen. But people watching was something she could handle, even enjoy.

About twenty minutes later as Grayson and Luna chatted at a table, the first round of rowdy guys arrived. They seemed younger than the military guys, not to mention they all had shaggy hair and were trailed by a group of girls dressed like they were going clubbing. They didn't seem to fit in with the laid-back scene of the bar.

"College kids," Luna explained, seeing Grayson's raised eyebrow. "They come here to get wasted before going round to the clubs. The drinks are cheaper at this bar."

"There's a college nearby?" Grayson asked, intrigued. If that was the case, she could look into taking classes. If she decided to stay, anyway.

"Yep. There is one right down the road."

"Is it a good one?"

Luna laughed. "I don't know. You're such a weirdo, Grayson."

They talked about an hour more, and Grayson was ready to call it a night, when the door slammed open. A group of men entered the bar.

Derrick was among them.

Grayson groaned out loud. Why did they keep crossing paths? The town was not that small. She watched as he scanned the room, and his eyes settled on hers. His expression didn't change. He stared a moment too long, and then followed the others to the bar.

"Isn't that the coffee shop guy?" Luna asked. Her lips quirked into a grin as she went on. "And Marcus?"

"Yep. What are the chances?"

"Pretty good, actually. This is the main bar where team guys hang out. I found out about it from Ethan."

Grayson fought the urge to groan again. This was all Luna's fault. "Can we go somewhere else? This isn't exactly a happening place."

"Patience."

"Didn't you tell me not to get involved with any local guys?"

"And you won't. Out-of-towners come here, too."

Sighing, Grayson asked, "How can you tell which is which?"

"Easy. Team guys come in small groups like that. Locals are loners sitting around the bar drowning their sorrows. Out-of-town guys travel in packs."

"Interesting. You always were the observant one."

"Speak of the devil." Luna took a swig from her beer as at least twenty guys filed into the bar. The noise level rose instantly.

Grayson snuck a peek at Derrick and was surprised to feel her blood boil when she saw a blonde girl sitting next to him, laughing at something he'd just said.

Grayson tore her gaze away and tapped her nails on the side of her glass.

The waitress set two drinks on the table and turned to point at the bar. "The guy with the baseball hat sent them."

Grayson looked at him. He was pretty big, close to six foot and stocky. She could feel Derrick's eyes on her. Picking up the beverage, she smiled at the large man before taking a drink.

Within minutes, the guy in the baseball hat and one of his friends were sitting across from them at their table. Grayson tried to keep up with the conversation,

but she kept glancing over at Derrick. Several times their eyes met, but he didn't come over or even bother to acknowledge her with a wave. The blonde was glued to his side, though he didn't seem to be too into her. He seemed more interested in what was happening at Grayson's table.

Now that excited her, more than she was willing to admit.

When their eyes met for what felt like the tenth time, Grayson excused herself to the restroom. She stopped by Derrick's table on the way. "Hey, Marcus."

"Hello, Ethan's incredible hot sister who is off-limits to us. Times two." He grinned.

Grayson laughed. "Where is my big brother anyway?" She snuck a peek at Derrick.

Beside him, the blonde narrowed her eyes and draped an arm over Derrick as if staking her claim. Without missing a beat, he picked up her arm and put it back down on the table. The girl looked like she was about to blow a gasket.

"He doesn't come out too often," Derrick responded. "He's a family man and all that. Who're your friends?" He tilted his head towards the table where Luna flirted with their guests.

"No idea." Grayson shrugged and continued towards the bathroom. Her heart was pounding against her chest. What the hell was it about that guy that caused her heart to go into overdrive?

She used the bathroom quickly, and stared at herself in the mirror as she washed her hands. An image of Derrick's eyes and sardonic smile was burned into her, and she couldn't shake him. It was one meeting in a cafe, and he made her come unglued. She needed to pull herself together.

She dried her hands and wrapped her hair into a bun before she stepped outside.

Derrick stood waiting for her, and she wasn't really surprised. She took him in. Like before, he looked strong and confident. He was wearing a button down plaid shirt rolled up over his powerful forearms and tan cargo pants. He looked like he belonged in one of those outdoor magazines. Once again, she had a flash of his hands on her body, and she forced her eyes back to his face.

"You really should be careful around strange men." His voice was passive, but ran with an undercurrent of something she couldn't decipher.

"Oh? Like yourself, you mean?"

He took a step closer. Her pulse raced. Was he going to kiss her? She couldn't believe how badly she wanted him to. Instead, he reached around and undid her bun, allowing her hair to fall around her shoulders.

"It looks better down."

Grayson touched her hair, unsure what to say or do. "Thanks, I guess."

"Be careful, Grayson."

Grayson looked into his serious green eyes, and before she could think it over, before she could stop the words from spilling out, she said, "Let's get out of here. Together."

Derrick's gaze locked on hers. She hated how his eyes seemed to look deep inside her, like he would catch a glimpse of the insecurity she was trying desperately to hide. "I don't think that's a good idea."

"Why not? Is it your girlfriend out there? I thought you didn't do serious?"

He didn't acknowledge her dig. "All the guys from

the team are here. Ethan would find out before we walked out the door."

She'd forgotten about her brother. Not that she really cared what he thought, but it brought her back to reality. She really didn't want to get involved with anyone this soon. It would be crazy. This was supposed to be her experimental phase, nothing long term. Hell, as far as she was concerned, she didn't want to start anything with anyone local, just passing through strangers.

"What happened to screw the rules?" Grayson asked.

Derrick gave her a lazy grin. His hands were now in his pockets, and he appeared relaxed and casual. It irked her, for some reason. She was a ball of nerves around him, and he was as cool as a cucumber.

"I work with your brother—life or death situations. I'd rather not piss him off. But, if you call me, we can definitely get together tomorrow."

"Ah, Derrick." Grayson reached for false bravado, leaning against the wall and holding a hand up. "You hesitated and lost. I guess I'll have to go home with Jerry."

His body remained relaxed, but she saw the twitch in his tightened jaw. "Your call."

"I asked you first," Grayson said and walked away. What the hell was she doing? It was like some alien had invaded her body. She took a deep breath and headed back to the table. Luna had wandered off to the pool table with Steve, leaving Jerry waiting for her.

Great.

"Your sister told me if I made you laugh, you'd let me take you home."

"What?" Grayson was so caught off guard by the

bold statement that she actually did laugh. Her sister never ceased to surprise her.

"Yeah, she said you have an off sense of humor, and if I wanted to take you home, making you laugh was the way to do it."

"My sister is crazy. But I guess she's right. I do like to laugh, and I do have an unusual sense of humor."

Jerry launched into a long, ridiculous joke that wasn't even funny, but it amused her that he tried. She just smiled and shook her head at him.

Grayson eyed the guy sitting across from her. He wasn't overly attractive, but not too bad looking either. Average, really. He had brown hair and light brown eyes. His nose was slightly too large and crooked. He obviously spent a lot of time at the gym, so he had that going for him, and he was attempting to be funny. Could she really have sex with this guy? She knew nothing about him.

Another glance at Derrick did the trick. By this point, the blonde was practically sitting on his lap, and he didn't seem to be pushing her away. His attention was focused on the chick.

Disappointment filled Grayson. Instead of moping, she decided she might as well have a little fun.

It was reckless, and she knew it. Leaning in, she yelled over the music. "Where are you staying?"

Jerry grinned. "At a hotel within walking distance from here."

Grayson grabbed her drink and downed the rest of it. "Let's go."

"Seriously?"

"Seriously."

He grasped her hand and led her past Derrick. They locked eyes, but he didn't say anything. Grayson waved at her sister who tilted her head back and laughed.

Grayson was now on the way to her second one-night stand within two weeks. Part of her wanted to tell him she'd changed her mind, but a bigger part of her thought, what the hell. Even her own mother said she was only young once.

They walked through the front door of the hotel and the woman behind the counter gave a knowing glance. More like a glance of disapproval.

Whatever. She's probably just jealous.

"My room's a mess. I wasn't expecting to bring anyone back." Jerry looked embarrassed as they walked down the hall.

"I don't care."

He pushed the door open. He wasn't exaggerating. The room was a mess, but at least the bed was made. It was somewhat reassuring that he hadn't gone to the bar to pick someone up.

The door closed loudly behind them.

They stood in awkward silence for a moment. Grayson thought about bolting. Finally, he took a step forward, and his hand slipped behind her hair, his thumb rubbing the base of her neck.

His lips met hers and he wrapped his arms around her, pulling her close. *Where was the sense of excitement?* Grayson wondered. Their clothes quickly dropped to the floor.

Jerry stood back to take her in. "Beautiful," he whispered. She didn't even feel self-conscious since she knew she would never see him again.

His lips trailed down her neck. She closed her eyes. Derrick flashed through her mind, and her body tensed.

Jerry stopped. "Everything okay?"

She nodded and trailed her fingers down his muscular chest. Continuing down, Grayson's fingers slid over his hard cock and felt it twitch in her hand. It was crazy how much power women had over men when it came to sex. One look, one move or touch was all it took to make them go crazy.

He began to use his tongue to descend down her body, devouring her as if he never tasted anything so good. Why wasn't she into it? She needed to focus. She wasn't going to let Derrick ruin her night. He took up way too much of her mental time as it was.

She leaned into Jerry before they tumbled onto the bed. His large hand squeezed her breast as he wrapped his tongue around her nipple and sucked hard. Her body finally responded, her back arching as she moaned softly.

Grayson went through the motions, but wasn't able to climax. Her mind kept wandering to Derrick. Jerry seemed to enjoy himself though. That should have counted for something.

The sex was just okay. Nothing earth shattering, and once again, she left without exchanging contact information. She should have felt like a whore, but instead she felt confused—confused by the fact that she let Derrick cloud her chance of no strings attached sex with a man who clearly wanted her.

Grayson rubbed the back of her neck, her muscles tight with tension.

Maybe it wasn't really Derrick. She could blame the call from Joshua instead. Her mind just wasn't where it should have been in the heat of the moment. Her emotions were all over the place, so of course she wasn't into it.

A. J. BENNETT

It had nothing to do with a certain rusty-haired guy who kept unexpectedly showing up and causing the ground to lurch beneath her.

Right?

CHAPTER 15

The next morning, Grayson's mom left early to run errands, and she was alone in the house. At any other time, she would have loved the solitude. Today, however, she had way too much on her mind.

It started with a phone call while she was cleaning up the kitchen after breakfast. The first ring tore through the silence like an alarm. Grayson put down the towel she was using to wipe the counter and slowly made her way to the phone. She paused, her hand hovering indecisively over the cordless phone nestled in its base. Three rings later, she was glad she hadn't answered.

"Grayson. Baby. Please come home." Josh's smooth voice filtered through the answering machine. "I can't live without you. I need y—"

On a wave of hot rage, Grayson slammed a finger to the "stop" button and cut off his message mid-sentence.

How dare he call here again begging for her to come back? Had their conversation the day before not been enough to prove she was serious? Grayson stomped down the hall and jerked open the closet door, removing her mother's fancy, ball bearing vacuum cleaner. The obnoxious whir of the machine had to be better than her own thoughts. She needed something to drown out the endless clutter in her brain.

She started with the bedrooms, tediously moving furniture and picking up cat toys as she moved along. She tried not to think about Josh and what would happen if he showed up. However, trying not to think of Josh made her obsess on the awkward sex she'd had the night before, which wasn't a better train of thought.

Jerry wasn't a bad guy. He was actually pretty nice and a bit attractive. Between Derrick's random appearance at the bar and Josh's phone call, Grayson never had a chance to truly enjoy herself.

Twenty minutes later, the living room floor was done, and Grayson felt better. She decided to go one step further and vacuum beneath the couch cushions. It wasn't that her mother was dirty, per se. She could clean with the best of them. But she wasn't *thorough*. She didn't get the nooks and crannies, which meant dust bunnies often accumulated beneath counters and furniture, and the couch cushions tended to collect coins, pens, and various other items nobody ever missed.

Grayson lifted the first cushion and removed long lost items—one of which was the small remote control to her mom's stereo—and then used the hose to vacuum the corners. When she moved to the second cushion, she froze, staring down at old, faded receipts, a dollar fifty in change...

... And a Starbucks sleeve with Derrick's number scrawled across it.

She picked it up and stared at it for a long moment. She'd completely forgotten about shoving it in the cushions the day after she arrived in town. Why had she kept it? She wasn't going to call. Before she talked herself out of it, she tossed it into the trashcan and returned to her cleaning.

But, she didn't even make it halfway through dusting the living room. It was like the damn coffee sleeve was calling her name. Sighing, she put down her rag and can of aerosol wood cleaner.

Don't do it.

Grayson took a deep breath, walked back over to the trash, and grabbed the sleeve out of it. Obviously, self-control was not one of her strong suits.

She had a feeling she was going to regret it, but she couldn't seem to stop herself. Flopping down on the couch, she pulled her phone out of her pocket. Before she could change her mind, she quickly dialed his number. It rang three times, and she was about to hang up when his clear voice came across the line.

"Hello?"

Say something, you idiot.

"Umm, hey. It's Grayson."

She was met with silence. Did he really not remember her?

"Umm, you know, Ethan's sister?" she went on, cringing at how upset she sounded. He was a complete stranger, she told herself. Of course he didn't remember her.

"I know who you are." There was nothing in his voice to show her he was happy to hear from her. If anything, he sounded gruff and distracted.

Horrified, Grayson spoke in a rush. "I shouldn't have called. Sorry." She hung up the phone before the

entire word "sorry" even came out of her mouth.

I'm such an idiot, Grayson thought to herself, jumping when she heard her phone ring.

It rang within seconds of her hanging up on Derrick. She hesitated then answered.

"Why did you hang up on me?" Derrick asked, amusement lacing his tone.

"You didn't seem like you wanted to talk."

There was a slight edge to his voice when he spoke again. "Did you have fun the other night?"

"Probably as much fun as you had."

"I kinda doubt that. I went home alone and you, well, you kinda did the opposite."

"I'm sure your girlfriend was disappointed."

"She's not my girlfriend. I thought I told you that."

"Oh. Well, you might want to tell her that then." Had she really misread the situation?

"Why did you call me?"

"I don't know. Well, I do, but it's stupid. You'll probably laugh at me."

"Try me."

"I don't really know how to explain it." She paused, gathering her nerve and blew out a breath. "What you saw the other night—that's not me, but I feel like it's becoming me. And I don't like it, or maybe I like it too much. I'm not sure which."

"What do you mean?" She could hear the curiosity in his voice.

Her stomach twisted as she continued. Her mind was rapidly trying to sort through her thoughts to get the right words out. "I moved here, because I was getting out of a bad relationship, and now well, I'm... turning into my sister."

"What does this have to do with me?"

"Well, that's where the crazy part comes in." She took a deep breath and then the words that had been playing over and over in her head tumbled from her lips. "I'm obviously attracted to you, and I was hoping it might be mutual so, I was thinking we could maybe have sex. And if it was good, we could continue, and I wouldn't end up leaving with strange men I met at bars. If it wasn't … enjoyable I mean, maybe we could just be friends?"

Had she really just said that out loud? Her pulse raced while she waited for his response.

The line went silent for a moment, and then Derrick said, "Okay."

CHAPTER 16

Excitement raised goose bumps on Grayson's arms. "Okay? You don't think I'm insane?"

"Well, this is definitely a first for me," Derrick said with a laugh. The sound brought a smile to her face. "And yeah, it's a little crazy."

Grayson couldn't argue with him on that point. She was still reeling that she'd even suggested such a thing.

"We'd need some rules though," Grayson said. She wanted to get that out in the open before anything happened between them. If they set up boundaries, this would work better.

"Rules huh...Such as? I'm not a big fan of rules. After all, if I was I wouldn't be having this conversation with you right now."

"No falling in love."

Derrick laughed.

"I'm serious. I'll just hurt you. I can't do a real relationship right now or maybe ever. No dating. No romance. Just sex, and maybe friendship. You know, the whole cliché *friends with benefits* thing."

"I'm coming to pick you up," he said, not acknowledging any of what she just said.

"Yes now, before you change your mind. What's your address?"

Grayson rattled off the address, her heart in overdrive. Her knees felt like they might buckle.

"Alright." Grayson hung up the phone and wondered once again what the hell she had gotten herself into. Realizing her limited timeframe before he was likely to arrive, and the fact that she probably stunk from obsessively cleaning the house, she ran into the bathroom jumped in the shower and rinsed off quickly. Grayson never brushed her teeth so thoroughly in her life. She then changed into a bra and panties that matched. She sprayed on a woodsy perfume, her hands shaking the entire time.

What if Derrick was a dud like Jerry, and Todd was an anomaly? That would be awkward. What if her brother found out? He would be so pissed.

Whatever, Grayson told herself, laughing out loud. She was a grown woman. She didn't have to listen to her older brother.

By the time Derrick pulled up in a black SUV, eagerness and a low simmering of excitement had started to make her feel like a live wire.

Grayson ran out the door before he had a chance to get out of the car. This arrangement needed to be purely about the sex. No boyfriend-type moves like opening her car door were going to happen as far as she was concerned.

"Hey," she said breathlessly, meeting him at the passenger door.

Derrick just lifted an eyebrow with a slight twinkle in his eye and opened the door for her.

Damn it, Grayson thought. *There goes that plan.*

The sleeves of his cotton shirt were pushed up, revealing his muscular forearms. He looked even more handsome then she remembered, if that was possible. She wanted him bad, and now.

Grayson slid into the seat, wiping her sweaty hands on her jeans as he closed the door behind her. This had to be the craziest thing she'd ever done in her life. Well, maybe not the craziest thing, but close to it. All of the wild moments in her life seemed to be increasing since leaving Josh. She didn't know if that was a good thing or a bad thing.

Grayson needed to mentally check herself. *Whatever,* she told herself. *Just go with it, and shut your damn brain off already.*

Derrick put the SUV in drive and then took off down the road. They sat in an uncomfortable silence for a few moments. She looked out the window and watched as they passed rows of houses and a blur of colorful, fall trees. Finally, Derrick broke the ice, and Grayson couldn't help but let out a small sigh of relief.

"So tell me, Grayson. What do you do with your free time?"

It was a positive sign that he asked about her. Unlike most guys who liked to talk about themselves. "I don't know. Read, hike, and other lame stuff. Nothing very exciting." Ugh, she was such a dork.

He glanced at her. "I love to read, too."

Grayson remembered. He'd had his face buried in a book in the coffee shop the day he'd scribbled his name and number on her cup. "Really? Who's your favorite author?" Grayson asked. A person's favorite author told a lot about them.

"That's a hard question to answer." Derrick paused, thinking. Her eyes went to the one hand tossed lazily over the steering wheel. "But a gun to my head, I would have to say Dostoyevsky."

"Really? I loved The Brothers Karamazov." She was impressed. No mainstream, millionaire modern author for this man.

They fell silent.

Derrick cleared his throat. "So where did you move here from?"

Grayson turned to the side to look at him. He had a great profile, and she wanted to run her hand down his jaw line. But, she resisted. "Arizona. I was going to college there the last three years."

"Why did you move?"

"I'd rather not talk about that."

"Fair enough." His eyes went back to the road.

"I was pretty surprised you called me."

"Me, too. I honestly don't know why I did. I mean I know why, I just don't know what came over me. Like I said I don't usually do this type of thing."

"Chemistry," he said simply.

She unconsciously licked her lips, her body tingling.

"Chemistry?"

"Sure, once in a while, two people meet and there's instant chemistry. It's natural to want to explore it."

"I guess that makes sense." Grayson pulled her sleeves down to cover her palms. "So you're saying you felt it too?"

"Of course I felt it. Wasn't that obvious?"

"Not really. You're kind of standoffish actually."

"Am I?"

"Yeah, a little bit." It was that trait that made her want to learn more about him.

"Do you feel it often? I mean with a lot of other women?"

"Chemistry? Nope, it wouldn't be as appealing if it wasn't rare."

That's true. There were tons of attractive guys out there, but she was rarely as drawn to someone through mere eye contact alone.

Derrick flicked on the blinker and pulled into a hotel. Grayson was caught off guard. Her gaze flew to his face. "A hotel?"

"I have a roommate."

"Or a girlfriend," Grayson said with a shrug. "If you have a girlfriend, that's fine. I told you this wasn't going to be serious."

Derrick sighed, pulling into a parking spot. "I don't have a girlfriend. I'm staying with a guy on the team, and they have a kid. I don't think it's appropriate to have sex in their house, and Ethan told me you were living with your mom."

Grayson nodded, strangely relieved to have an explanation. She really didn't want to mess around with a guy who was already seeing somebody. There was too much baggage involved, too much room for error.

"I'm going to go get a room. Wait here." He didn't give her time to answer before he jumped out and went inside.

To say she was nervous would be an understatement. The other times she'd thrown caution to the wind and jumped into bed with strangers, at least she'd been drinking. She could use some liquid courage that was for sure.

Derrick walked around the vehicle and opened her door. Her heart felt like it was going to jump out of her chest.

This time, it was the middle of the day, and she was sober as could be.

CHAPTER 17

They stepped through the doorway, and Grayson looked around, taking in the room. It was pretty nice. It smelled clean and was full of light from the big picture window. The bed was king-sized, covered in pillows and a comforter in a demure shade of lavender.

Grayson stepped out of her shoes, padding in bare feet over the soft carpet until she could see out the window. The glistening blue jewel of the outdoor swimming pool was below the room. She was surprised it was still open for the season. Grabbing the rod, Grayson moved to close the curtains.

"Leave it." Derrick's words fell into the room.

Her hand dropped, and she looked over at him in surprise. His back was to her as he shrugged out of his jacket.

"I like the light," he explained without turning. He took off his watch and dropped it onto the nightstand with a thud. "Take off your clothes."

Heat rose to Grayson's cheeks. She really didn't know what to expect, but she hadn't been expecting that. It sounded so impersonal—detached almost.

Grayson tried not to let it get to her.

He turned to look at her. His voice was barely above a whisper as he repeated, "Take them off."

Grayson shifted back and forth on her feet, uncomfortable beneath Derrick's hard, green gaze. What the hell had she gotten herself into? She could feel the pulse in her neck beating too fast.

"Grayson. You called me, remember?"

He was right. She knew exactly what they were going to do, so it shouldn't have come as a surprise. But she still shivered as she gripped the hem of her shirt and peeled it off, Derrick watching her every move. She shimmied out of her jeans, kicking them to the side.

Derrick's lips quirked as his eyes shifted to her chest. "All of it."

Grayson fumbled with her bra, her hands trembling as she freed her breasts to the chill air of the hotel room. The feeling of his gaze on her naked torso sent heat straight to her core. She slid off her panties, trying to act like it was no big deal, but she had never felt so exposed in her life. She had to force her hands to stay at her sides instead of covering her breasts.

The room was so quiet, too quiet. She wished there was music playing or something else to fill the silence. As if the room had heard her thoughts, the air conditioner kicked on. The soft hum relaxed her.

Derrick was still fully clothed. She crossed the room slowly, feeling extremely vulnerable under his intense but approving gaze. He watched her as if she was a piece of art on display, and it made her nervous as hell.

Every step took her closer to him, yet he didn't move an inch. He stood with his hands at his sides, his body lazy and confident. Grayson suddenly had an overwhelming feeling she'd bit off more than she could chew with this man.

With her heart nearly in her throat, Grayson pressed her body to his.

He reacted immediately, one strong hand moving to cup her butt, jerking her against him possessively. His thumb glided across her bottom lip, the touch of his finger felt like fire. Too fleeting as his hands fell away.

Derrick tugged off his shirt, exposing his broad, muscled chest. Grayson's hands shook as she traced her palms over his rippled stomach, her back arching so that her breasts flattened against his hot skin.

Her fingers fumbled over his pants. She was determined not to let him see how nervous she was, but it took her three tries to open his pants.

Standing on her tippy toes, Grayson kissed him slowly at first, and he responded with urgency, his fingers tangling in her hair. He tasted like cinnamon, and smelled masculine and earthy. His body was warm and firm against hers.

Breaking the kiss, Derrick turned her so she was facing the mirror, and then kicked off his pants. He drew close, his hard body a long line against her back. Slowly, he pulled her hair to the side. She closed her eyes and sighed as his warm lips brushed her shoulder. One of his legs nudged her foot, spreading her legs.

A thrill shot through her as the weight of his body pressed her forward, bending her over the table. She grasped the edge of the wood, her breath uneven. His hand trailed down her neck, going lower until he reached her breast. Her chest heaved as he rolled her nipple between his fingers, causing her body to tingle.

She was already wet before his other hand strayed and began to caress her. His fingers were gentle and expert. She heard herself making noises in her throat, completely at the will of his touch.

Breath ragged, Grayson waited. She groaned as his fingers plunged inside of her. His teasing was driving her mad, and she didn't know how much more she could take. She tried to turn around, but he pressed his body harder against hers. He was in complete control, and he knew it. Sex was the one area she always felt the need to have some control, so this was new to her.

He lowered his head, his warm tongue on her neck, and then made his way to her ear. "What do you want?" he whispered.

Their eyes met in the mirror, and what she saw in his green-eyed gaze made her stomach flutter. His lips softly touched the nape of her neck, causing her to lose what little self-control she had left. She watched through the mirror as his hands inched up her stomach to her breasts, moving slowly in circular caresses. Every nerve in her body felt like it was on fire.

"Grayson, I asked you a question," he murmured into her ear.

"You, Derrick," Grayson whimpered, hating herself because she knew it was true. "I need you. Please."

He grabbed her hips with his warm calloused hands and slid inside her. Slowly. Inch by inch, he opened her and filled her. She closed her eyes, a moan in her throat.

Derrick wrapped his hand around her long hair and pulled her head up. "Don't close your eyes. Watch."

Her eyes snapped open. Her face was flushed red and her eyes bright. She was surprised to be so turned on by the sight. Gripping the edge of the table, Derrick began moving within her, his body hovering above hers. Grayson watched her chest bounce with each thrust.

"Oh, God, Derrick," she gasped out.

Urged on by her throaty moans, he thrust deeper. Her whole body shivered, her legs shaking in pleasure as the orgasm built. Derrick gripped her hips, moving harder, faster, until stars burst in Grayson's world, and she spiraled into climax.

Derrick pulled her back, and they tumbled onto the bed. In one quick movement, he rolled her on top of him. She stared down at his face as she lowered herself onto him. Her hair spilled all around him, and his hand grasped the back of her neck, getting tangled in her hair. He pulled her lips to meet his.

Breathless, she broke free from the kiss and leaned back.

She slid her palm over his chest. His skin was taut over his hard muscles. God, he was so sexy, it was amazing. She rocked her hips slowly and leaned down, her lips finding his once again. Her taut nipples were sensitive to the friction of rubbing back and forth on his skin.

In the blink of an eye, Derrick was back on top and trailing his warm tongue down her neck. His tongue circled her nipple, and then moved down to her belly button as she squirmed from pure pleasure beneath his mouth. He worked his way down until his lips were on her inner thigh. Grayson closed her eyes and groaned in anticipation.

Grayson moaned and lifted her hips. "Derrick,

please."

He slid an arm under her thigh and pulled her closer. His mouth left her leg, and his warm tongue slowly trailed along her core, while his expert fingers teased her at the same time. Talk about stimulation overload. The man she barely knew had the ability to make her insane with desire. Grayson's moans got even louder, her legs trembling as another orgasm ripped through her. She relaxed, legs falling to the side with a satisfied smile.

"I've wanted to taste you since the day we met," Derrick said gruffly, moving up her body on his hands and knees. His lips met hers in a deep kiss, and then he leaned back, threw her legs on the crook of his arms, and buried himself deep inside.

Grayson gasped at the penetration, her head sinking into the pillow as she rode his movements. She met him thrust for thrust, her skin slick with sweat against his. Derrick moved faster, his eyes drifting shut momentarily before he let out a primal growl and climaxed.

Heart beating fast, Grayson could hardly move. Derrick rolled off of her, his weight disappearing so fast it left her bereft. They lay next to each other, catching their breath.

Finally, Derrick grinned, running his fingers lightly up her arm. "So? Did I pass the test?"

She stretched, rolling onto her side. "With flying colors." In the moment of silence that followed, Grayson studied him. She felt a pang of some emotion she feared exploring. There was no way she could let herself fall for this guy. Her sister-in-law swore he was a heartbreaker, and just by looking at him, Grayson agreed. "Look. We need some more ground rules."

"I'm not sure I like the sound of that," he said warily. "More rules?"

"We just had sex without protection. If you want to have sex with me again, there will be some rules."

"OK, let's hear them."

"Number one: If you have sex with anyone else, you need to use a condom."

He raised an eyebrow. "And you? How do I know you'll use protection?"

"I'm on the pill, but if I have sex with anyone else—which, I probably will—I promise I'll use condoms."

"What else?" he asked, running his fingers along the crook of her waist.

She shivered under his touch. "Do you have a girlfriend? I don't care if you do, but I don't want to be taken by surprise either."

"No girlfriend." His eyes met hers, and he looked sincere, but there was still a little nagging voice in the back of her head telling her that he was lying. She had learned long ago to listen to the little voice in her head, but she wanted to believe him.

"If you get one, we're done."

"OK. I guess. That doesn't really make sense, but I'll go with it for now." Derrick continued to trace his fingers up her forearm. "Anything else on your rule list?"

"I'm sure there is, but you make it hard to think." Grayson sighed. "I'm going to be sore as hell tomorrow."

"So tell me, Gray. Where do I fall in your long line of conquests?"

Grayson grinned. "Did you just call me Gray?"

"You don't like to be called Gray?"

"Actually, I love it. As a kid, I insisted that everyone called me Gray instead of Grayson, but no one listened

except my grandmother."

"You're avoiding the question."

Grayson propped her head in her hand and stared at his profile. "No, I'm not. I'm thinking about it. I'm not sure I should inflate your ego so early on."

"You don't have to lie. I'm a big boy."

"I haven't been with very many people."

Derrick looked at her, his expression saying, "Yeah, right."

"I'm serious. Up until three weeks ago, I had only been with one guy. And since then, I've had two one night stands."

"Really?" His attention was fully on her now. "Were you and your ex high school sweethearts?"

"We might as well have been. I met him during the first year of college, and didn't really date in high school. Other than that loser, Chase, who felt me up at a dance, and then went out with my sister the next day."

"You expect me to believe you were a virgin until college?"

"I don't expect you to believe anything, but it's the truth. I've always lived in my sister's shadow. That's the way I like it, too." Grayson turned and stared at a water spot on the ceiling.

"You certainly don't seem very inexperienced." Derrick's hand caressed her stomach, and she could see he was clearly aroused once again.

"Just because I haven't been with many people doesn't mean I haven't had a lot of sex. It was just with the same person."

"On a scale of one to four, where do I fall?" Derrick was now on top of her and had her hands pinned above her head.

Grayson's breath hitched. She wasn't about to tell him that just his touch was enough to drive her crazy, or that when his warm lips touched her skin, she was like putty in his hands. He made her want to forget that Todd, Jerry, and Josh had ever laid a hand on her. She couldn't tell him that three years of sex with Josh couldn't even come close to one night with him.

She smiled coyly. "I'd say you're number two."

"Number two, huh? I guess I have to work a little harder."

CHAPTER 18

The next day, while driving back from the grocery store, Grayson's phone rang. Her eyebrow rose in surprise when she saw it was Derrick. Just the sight of his name across the screen made her stomach drop. She pulled into the driveway hitting the brakes too hard causing a bag to spill on the floor. She frowned as she watched an apple roll under the passenger seat.

Taking a deep breath she answered, "Hey, didn't expect to hear from you so soon."

"Why's that?"

"I don't know."

Maybe because you're a womanizer, she thought.

"I was just calling to see how your day was going."

"Really? You just called to see how my day was?" A wide smile spread across her face as she grabbed the items that had been fallen out and threw them back in the bag.

"Yes. Really is there something wrong with that?" He chuckled.

"I guess not. I'm just surprised."

"Well, I can hang up if that would make you feel

better?"

Grayson laughed. "No, don't do that. My day has been fine. Yoga in the morning, then I took my Jeep to get an oil change and got groceries for my mom. How about you?"

"Good. I'm on lunch break now. I thought I'd say hello and let you know I enjoyed yesterday."

"Me, too."

"We'll have to do it again soon."

"Are you asking to see me today?" Grayson immediately wanted to take back those words. *Desperate much, Grayson? Get it together, play it cool.*

"Not today. I'll call you tomorrow."

"Oh. Okay then. I guess I'll talk to you later." Grayson clicked off the phone, feeling like an idiot. She had a feeling this was going to get complicated real quick. The fact that he called so soon kind of freaked her out, but also made her way happier than it should have. Perhaps he saw her as more than someone to just hook up with. Or maybe he was just a nice guy and calling the day after was out of respect. She scolded herself. She was pathetic and had no idea how to even act around guys. She wished she could talk to Luna about it, but she was keeping Derrick to herself.

She pushed the Jeep door open and grabbed the rest of the groceries from the back.

No strings attached Gray, she said over and over under her breath.

A couple of hours later, Grayson was blissfully soaking in the tub, the scent of lavender soothing her nerves when her phone vibrated. Derrick's name flashed across the screen, and she reached for the phone dropping it on the floor with her wet hands. Ugh, she could just get back to him after the bath. She leaned backward and rested her head against the tub. Who was she kidding, seconds later she caved. It was driving her crazy; she wanted to know what he had to say. Pulling herself out of the tub she slipped and knocked her chin on the edge of the tub.

Seriously! That freaking hurt!

The coppery taste of blood filled her mouth as she rubbed her chin blinking back tears, and grabbed the phone.

I changed my mind. I want to see you.

Grayson decided that a text back would be a better option than calling, after nearly knocking herself unconscious.

When? I'm kinda busy at the moment. She was trying to play it off that she wasn't going to jump when he called, but she was dying to see him again. Even as her chin throbbed in pain, he was all she could think about.

I see. So I guess you don't want to go hiking?

She loved to be in the woods. Had she told him she liked hiking? She couldn't remember. *Actually, that sounds amazing. When?*

I'm outside your door.

What? Give me a minute. I'm in the tub. Grayson grabbed the towel and quickly dried her legs and arms. Thankfully, she had kept her hair up in a bun so it wasn't wet. She cupped her hands and rinsed water in her mouth to get rid of the taste of blood.

She pushed through the door and ran into her room to get dressed. She hadn't thought to bring her hiking boots with her, so she slipped on a pair of sneakers. With a quick glance in the mirror, her chin

didn't look swollen; she turned, grabbed her jacket and strode to the front door. Derrick was standing there with his hands in his pockets looking completely at ease with himself. She wanted to rip off his shirt and pull him into the house.

"A little notice would have been nice." Grayson huffed. She quickly softened when he shrugged and said with the faintest hint of a twinkle in his green eyes.

"I was in the neighborhood."

"Uh. Huh."

Maybe he wanted to see her again as much as she wanted to see him. That thought was frightening. What the hell could the chances be that she met someone the first day in Tennessee at a coffee shop? It was completely absurd and he was already messing with her plans of being single. Going hiking felt like a date to her.

"Ready?"

That's when she noticed the motorcycle. "You've got a motorcycle?"

"I hope that's ok?"

"Of course it is. Ethan used to sneak us around the neighborhood on his when we were younger. He'd push it out of the driveway so my mom wouldn't hear. It's been ages since I've been on one."

"Well let's rectify that right now."

Grayson looked behind her and grabbed her sunglasses off the bookshelf.

Derrick walked her to the bike and handed her an extra helmet.

He took a step closer and ran his hand down her arm. "When I was driving home from work I had a sudden flash of fucking you up against a tree."

At a loss for words, Grayson just stared at him, praying she wasn't as red in the face as she felt. Okay, so maybe he wasn't thinking of this as a date. Finally, she recovered and managed to get out. "I've never had sex outside before."

"Well that's even better. We'll have to see how many firsts we can cross of your list."

Grayson grinned, aroused by his words. She put the helmet on. It was too big, but she cinched it as tight as it would go. She climbed on back and wrapped her arms around his waist. Her chest pressed against his back. Did life get any better than this?

Derrick turned the key and kicked the throttle. The bike lurched forward, and Grayson held on tighter pressing her cheek against his back. She felt free and happy with the wind on her face.

Derrick turned down a long winding road flanked with beautiful golden trees. He pulled off to the side of the road and turned off the engine, she jumped off, handing him the helmet.

"Is this where you take all the girls?" She looked around. It was beautiful and quiet.

"Nope. Only you, Gray."

She wondered if they were really going to have sex, or if he was just teasing her. Either way it was nice to be outside, so she decided to just go with it. The cool crisp fall air felt wonderful against her skin. Golden leaves floated around them bringing a smile to her lips.

There wasn't a path. Derrick walked ahead and held the branches back so they wouldn't smack her in the face. Twigs loudly crunched under her feet in the still air. Eventually, they reached a walking trail surround by towering oak trees. It was relatively quiet,

but occasionally a runner would pass them. They walked for about a mile in comfortable silence.

Without warning Derrick grabbed her hand and pulled her deeper off the beaten path. Her heart felt like it was going to explode in her chest. Having sex with someone she barely knew was crazy; having sex outside where people ran in the middle of the day was completely insane. If she kept this up she was going to need to be committed or arrested for indecent exposure.

Grabbing her by the arm Derrick turned her around. His closed the distance between them, until his chest was pressed against hers and she could feel his heart beating strong and steady. He seemed as nervous and excited as she was. His cool hand wandered under her shirt and unclasped her bra. His thumb brushed her nipple while his mouth found her neck. His touch made her weak in the knees. It was overwhelming, the feel of his warm mouth against her skin combined with the chilly air. He pushed her shirt to the side to expose her bare shoulder, and his lips trailed to her collarbone as he unbuttoned her pants. Grayson sighed.

"I love the sounds you make," Derrick murmured.

Grayson reached down, unzipped his pants and wrapped her hand around his thick, long cock, gliding her hand up and down. Her whole body quivered with urgency.

Derrick groaned, as he turned her around her hand dropped away from his hard cock. His hand ran down the curves of her body, stopping at her waist. She wanted him so badly. Any inhibition was thrown out the window. Smiling, she reached out and grabbed the tree, bending herself over. She heard his pants drop to the ground, and another moan escaped her mouth. There was something almost magical about having sex in the middle of nature. It was truly exhilarating, and one of the most exciting things she has ever done so far.

He reached around and put his fingers in her mouth. His breath upon her neck sent shivers down her spine. She rolled her tongue around his fingers, and sucked on them as if she were sucking on his cock. He grunted and pulled his hand away from her mouth, immediately reaching down, rubbing her clit. Slowly, he slid his cock into her, and she leaned back wanting all of him. His fingers dug into her hips as his pace became almost frantic. He plunged deep into her over and over again. When he felt her body shudder with an orgasm, he came quickly after, and pulled out before collapsing against her.

"Wow. That was—different." Grayson reached down to pull up her pants even though she wanted to collapse onto the ground. Her legs were shaking. Hell, her entire body was shaking.

"Wait." He pulled out a sanitary wipe from his jacket.

Grayson laughed. "Well, aren't you quite the Boy Scout."

"Something like that." He wiped her clean and then she pulled up her jeans.

Derrick was already dressed, his face flushed. The sex had been fast, but it was absolutely incredible. Just then, a runner passed by with a dog, causing them to look at each other and laugh. One minute earlier, the runner and his dog would have gotten to see a show. For a reason unknown to her, Grayson found herself excited thinking that they almost got caught.

Taking her hand, Derrick threaded his fingers through hers and led her back to the trail. Once they got back to the trail, he dropped her hand, and she looked over at him puzzled. She wanted to wrap her arm around his waist and pull him next to her, but that wasn't their relationship. She was surprised by how much it bothered her that he had dropped her hand. *Get a grip.*

She forced a smile and pretended it didn't hurt.

As they walked down the trail, Derrick glanced over at her.

"Tell me about your ex."

Random much? That was an odd thing for him to bring up. "Not much to tell. He was a jackass. It took a while for me to wake up to it, but I finally left him."

"And he just let you go?"

"He didn't know I left."

"Interesting."

"Not really. What about you? Any serious relationships or are you really just a man whore?" Grayson asked and couldn't keep the smile off her face.

Derrick glanced over at her and shook his head with a smile. "I had a serious relationship once. Thought she was the one, and then she cheated on me with one of my buddies."

"Ouch."

"Yeah, ouch is right. So, never again."

"So, a broken heart led you to become the cold heartless womanizer that you are today?"

"I guess you could say that," he said with a laugh. "I've never given it much thought."

"It looks like we're the ideal pair of dysfunction."

"Seems so," he grinned. Once again she felt like a schoolgirl.

CHAPTER 19

Grayson's body tensed when they turned down the road. A red Mustang was parked in her mom's driveway. "Oh shit." Grayson groaned and banged her head against his back. "This cannot be happening right now."

"What's wrong?" Derrick asked, turning his head.

"My ex!" Grayson yelled and pointed. "He's at my mom's house."

Derrick pulled over to the side of the road and cut the engine. "Do you think he'll cause trouble?"

Grayson shrugged and looked down at her hands. She felt very exposed under his concerned gaze. "He's got a temper and thinks I belong to him."

"Is that so?" Derrick gripped the handlebars tighter, causing his knuckles to turn white.

"So I have no idea who we will meet, Dr. Jekyll or Mr. Hyde."

"I'm coming in with you," he said firmly.

"No, you don't have to, it's not your problem. He's already going to freak out that I'm with a guy."

"Well, in that case I'm definitely coming in."

"You don't know him, Derrick. He's an asshole," she said softly.

He smiled and squeezed her thigh. "Hey, I'm a Green Beret. Remember?"

Grayson nodded her head once and tried to force a smile. She knew he was trying to lighten the mood, but her stomach was in knots. "Thanks." As much as she hated to admit it she was glad Derrick was there. Why did Josh have to show up? Couldn't he just leave her alone and let her get on with her life? Grayson felt like she was going to throw up. It went from the perfect day to the perfect storm in less than half an hour.

Derrick eased the bike back on the road, and towards Grayson's mother's house. Once he pulled onto the side of the road Grayson jumped off the motorcycle and pulled off the helmet. Derrick took it from her and latched it onto the back, and set his helmet on the seat. Adrenaline and fear fueled her every step.

As they walked forward, Josh stepped out of his car. His eyes darted from Grayson to Derrick and his face turned a dark shade of red, almost purple. She knew this was not going to end well and braced herself for the confrontation.

"What the fuck, Grayson?" Josh glared at her through narrowed eyes, his nostrils flared.

Ignoring his question, Grayson met his eyes. "I told you not to bother coming here. You wasted your money and time."

"Who the fuck is he?" Josh jerked his head towards Derrick. Grayson just rolled her eyes at his question, crossing her arms over her chest.

"I said who the fuck is he?" Josh practically

screamed.

Derrick stood silently beside her, his body relaxed. She felt somewhat comforted by his presence. Josh and Derrick were such a contrast to each other. She would never know what she had seen in Josh.

Josh's body was tense, and he looked like he was ready to explode. She should have known he would show up. It was too good to be true that he would just let her go so easily. He was crazy and obsessive, she felt stupid thinking he gave up just like that.

"I need to talk to you," Josh said through clenched teeth. " Alone."

Grayson shook her head. "Not going to happen. I told you we are done. Whatever you have to say, say it now, and then go."

Josh's fingers sunk into her arm with an iron grip, and he yanked her forward. She nearly stumbled on her face but managed to stay upright.

"Get your fucking hands off of her," Derrick said with an edge to his voice that made Grayson turn to look at him. His jaw was clenched and his stance had changed. Gone was the relaxed posture. He looked like he was ready to tear off Josh's head. His muscles were tense, and his weight had transferred to the balls of his feet. He looked like a wild animal awoken from a lazy nap, ready to pounce. For the first time, she saw the underlying danger Derrick kept quietly concealed.

Josh dropped his hand and took a step towards Derrick. Josh was not one to back down from a fight.

"You need to mind your own fucking business," Josh spat, his icy blue eyes wild.

"I think you need to leave, asshole. Gray has made it painfully obvious she doesn't want you here."

"Gray? He calls you fucking Gray?" Josh turned

to look at Grayson. "You're fucking this asshole? You moved on quickly didn't you? I knew it! I knew you were nothing more than a fucking slut."

"You need to go," Grayson glared at him and moved a step closer to Derrick.

"You heard her."

Josh let out a primal growl and lunged forward dropping his shoulder before he barreled into Derrick's midsection knocking him to the ground. What happened next was a blur of arms flying and the two of them rolling on the ground. Eventually, Derrick sprang to his feet, and Josh stumbled to stand. Derrick's lip looked swollen and Josh had blood pouring out of his nose.

Grayson stood watching in shock as they stalked each other in a circle. She should stop it, but part of her was enjoying seeing Josh getting some of his own medicine. She knew Derrick could hold his own, and then some. Two violent men—one wanted to hurt her and the other wanted to protect her.

Josh's fist came forward in a wild roundhouse punch that Derrick easily ducked.

"You're fucking pathetic," Derrick said in a low voice.

That just pissed off Josh even more. "I'm going to kill you," He growled, his face was contoured in rage.

Derrick laughed.

Josh advanced again and Derrick grabbed the back of his neck and pulled him forward slamming his knee into his sternum twice and then released him. Josh staggered backwards, and dropped to his knees gasping for air.

Grayson covered her mouth. "Enough," she screamed.

Derrick looked over at her and stepped back.

Josh was still kneeling on the ground his head bent. When he looked up, Grayson's eyes widened. He was a mess. His face was swollen his nose was clearly broken, and he was having trouble breathing.

"Derrick, maybe you should go."

"Not a chance. I'm not leaving here until he's gone." Derrick's chest heaved up and down. His green eyes met hers, and he winked. Grayson had to hide her smile. One small show of support from Derrick in a horrible situation calmed her.

Grayson walked over to Josh and knelt down next to him. "Please leave, Joshua. We're done, and you need to get on with your life. You should probably go to the hospital."

"Fuck you," he snapped and tried to stand, but fell forward. "You were my life you bitch." Tears glistened in his eyes.

"I'll get you some ice." Grayson stood up and brushed off her pants.

"I don't want your ice or anything else from you. I don't know why I wasted my time on you." He wiped blood off his face with the back of his sleeve. "You can go to hell for all I care. Both of you go to fucking hell!"

Josh spit blood onto the grass. "She's a good fuck isn't she? She's got that sweet, tight pussy, and she's always ready to go."

Grayson looked over at Derrick to see his reaction. His face was still. "Your loss is my gain. Now get your ass out of here before I call the cops."

Josh was able to get to his feet this time and stumbled to his car without looking back. The door was still open, and he fell into the seat and leaned his head on the steering wheel. He sat like that for at least ten minutes, before he shut the door and drove off. Grayson hoped it was the last time she would see him.

What a disaster.

When the car was out of site Grayson threw her arms around Derrick. "I'm sorry you had to get involved, but I am so glad you were here with me."

He brushed a strand of her hair behind her ear. "I despise guys like that. Only a coward would lay a hand on a woman."

She hated how vulnerable she felt, and she knew Derrick could see through her facade.

Leaning down he brushed his lips across her forehead. "You don't deserve that." He whispered and smoothed down her hair before his lips found hers. His kiss was soft and tender she could feel the tension leaving her body. When he winced Grayson pulled away and grabbed his hand. "Let's get you some ice. Your poor lip is swollen as hell."

"You should have seen the other guy." Derrick gave her a crooked grin that made her heart skip a few beats.

CHAPTER 20

Six days passed without so much as a text from Derrick. Though she'd never admit it out loud, Grayson missed him. A lot. Not hearing from him was driving her completely insane. She was an addict, and Derrick was her drug of choice. It was as if she was going through withdrawals with no word from him.

Pathetic.

She was certain that, after the incident with Josh, she and Derrick had crossed into new territory in their relationship. If anything, he pulled away more.

She felt like a complete fool for thinking it could be something more. He was constantly on her mind, and she ached to see him again. The rational part of her mind screamed for her to not get too deeply involved. Not that he was even giving her a chance to anyway. Nothing was going to come out of this relationship besides heartache. She just hadn't expected it to be her own.

She'd hoped they would make their sexual outings daily or at least every other day, but no, not as much as a phone call or a text. *What the hell?* She'd obviously read him completely wrong. When they walked to the door together, hand in hand, and he kissed her good-bye, she believed there had been more than just a sexual connection. She was even willing to toss aside her *no relationship* rule to give him a chance.

The front door swung open, and Luna breezed through without knocking. The door banged closed behind her. She looked hot, as usual. Her long hair flowed over her shoulders in soft curls, and her makeup was perfectly applied. The deep plum-colored shirt she was wearing was low cut and form fitting, accenting her curves. Grayson looked down at her own T-shirt and sweat pants. Her hair was pulled in a ponytail, and she didn't have a lick of makeup on. Sometimes she wished she was more into fashion like her sister, but it really didn't appeal to her. She would take comfort over style any day.

"Why aren't you dressed?" Luna demanded in a huff.

"I forgot you were coming over." Grayson sighed and stood up. She really didn't want to go out, but it was stupid to stay home and pine over a guy whom she told that she didn't want a relationship with. He certainly wasn't going out of his way to see her. The thought made her feel hollow inside. Obviously, she completely misread his feelings.

Such a fool, she repeated. "Where are we going this time?"

"Back to The Trap baby sister. We need some fresh blood."

"You need help." Grayson rolled her eyes.

"And you need to let your hair down and have a little fun."

"Yeah. Yeah. Give me a minute." Grayson made

her way down the hallway. Maybe she would run into Derrick again. She grabbed her phone and checked it for messages, but there was nothing. She hated herself, but she caved and texted him.

Hey, we're going to The Trap. Want to meet up?

She set the phone down and got dressed. A couple of minutes later it dinged. She caught herself bolting faster than she thought possible to get her phone to see his reply.

Sorry. Got plans, and I don't hang out at that place anyway.

Of course he had plans, probably a date.

K. Well have fun.

You too, Grayson. Be safe.

What had she expected? For him to jump at the chance to meet up with her? She was the one that set the ground rules. No dating, no exclusivity. He'd probably already grown bored with her and moved on. She went from being called Gray, back to being called Grayson. She was sure that he saw too much baggage to deal with. She couldn't blame him.

Grayson decided to take a bit more care in her appearance this time. She applied a hint of blush and lip gloss, and let her hair down. She settled on a form-fitting pale blue sweater and her favorite pair of faded jeans.

Grayson's head throbbed, and the room spun in circles around her when she tried to sit up. What had she done now?

She rested her head back on the pillow and squeezed her eyes shut willing her head to stop pounding. No such luck.

Hesitantly, she turned to the side and opened one eye expecting to see a stranger in bed beside her. Relief washed over her when she realized she was at her mother's in the spare room with the ugly quilt. Alone. She had no recollection of getting there. That was a bit of a problem. Glancing down, she realized she was only wearing her bra and panties.

Shit. Think, damn it! Grayson pinched the bridge of her nose. She really couldn't recall anything at all.

She tossed the covers off her and swung one leg off the edge of the bed and then the other. Gripping the sheets, she steadied herself before standing. For the life of her, she couldn't remember the last time she was this hung over. If she kept this up, she would need an intervention.

She grabbed her robe from the back of the computer chair and cinched it around her waist. She shuffled out the door and down the hall to the bathroom. Her head pounded with every step. The tile floor was cold beneath her bare feet, causing her to shiver.

Leaning against the sink, Grayson stared at her reflection. She looked like death warmed over. Her hair was a mess with random strands stuck to the sides of her face. The girl staring back at her was ghostly pale, and her eyes had dark circles underneath them. After splashing water on her face, Grayson made her way to the kitchen, and lowered herself into a chair.

"Who was that nice young man who brought you home last night?" Her mother asked, a little too loudly, with a twinkle in her eye as she set down a steaming mug of coffee. Instant of course, but on a day like this Grayson could care less.

Grayson groaned and dropped her head in her

hands. "I have no idea," she mumbled.

"He's a Taurus. I wouldn't let this one get away."

"Of course he is. Too bad I can't even remember his name, let alone what he looks like."

Her mother handed her two aspirins. Grayson popped them in her mouth and swallowed them down with coffee.

"You shouldn't drink that much. You never know what you could have missed out on."

"I'll try to remember that sage advice next time my evil twin drags me to a bar."

Her mother chuckled. "He looked awfully familiar." Her mom snapped her fingers. "Ethan's cookout. That's where I saw him."

Grayson's head snapped up fast enough that the room seemed to spin around her. "What did you say?"

"The young man. He's on Ethan's team. That was nice of him to bring you home. He even insisted on tucking you into bed. A real gentleman. You don't see them much these days."

"What did he look like?"

"Reddish hair, well built. Not bad looking at all."

"Where's my phone?" Grayson stood up and stumbled back to her room. How the hell could Derrick have brought her home? She didn't even remember seeing him. How much did she have to drink last night? What if she did something humiliating? Maybe someone slipped something in her drink.

Shit, Grayson, get it together.

She searched all over and couldn't find her phone. She probably lost it in her drunken haze. Could her morning get any worse?

"Your phone is on the TV stand," her mom yelled from the kitchen.

Grayson's head felt like it was going to explode. Every footstep echoed louder than someone banging pots together next to her ear. She grasped the phone and opened her messages. She cringed and dropped onto the loveseat. Damn it, she must have drunk texted Derrick. What was she back in high school? They really should have a "do not send this drunken text message" application for phones. That or someone needs to start leaving her phone at home before going out and making bad decisions.

Grayson took a deep breath and opened her text messages.

The first message she opened was from her to Derrick.

I can't stop thinking about your hands on my body.

She groaned inwardly and opened the reply from Derrick.

Is that so?

Yep. You're incredible. Ugh these idiots won't stop hitting on me.

That's what happens when you go to bars.

Come see me.

I told you I'm busy.

Date?

Does it matter?

I don't know...maybe?

Have fun Gray and be careful.

Fine.

Not as bad as it could have been, Grayson thought, starting to feel some relief. He called her Gray again, too, which she took as a good sign. Looking back down at her phone, she continued to try and put last night's events back together.

Two hours after their initial exchange, their

conversation continued.

Luna left me. I don't have any way home and I have no money for a cab. I'm way too drunk to drive. She had texted him.

So your solution is to text me at 0230?

Never mind. I'm sure one of these guys will take me back to their hotel. I don't even want to have sex right now. I can barely stand.

I'll be right there. Are you still at The Trap?

Yesssss. Thank you sooooooo much. xoxoxs

Grayson set the phone down and fell back into the couch. XOXOXs? Seriously? She put her head in her hands and shook her head.

How embarrassing.

So she texted Derrick, and he came to her rescue—again. She must have passed out on the drive back to her mom's house. Or maybe she was already passed out when he got there. It was without a doubt the most unattractive thing she could've done.

She grasped her phone. One of the crazy cats jumped on her lap, but she nudged it off the couch. Her head hurt too badly. She had to text Derrick and say thank you. It felt like some sort of fucked up walk of shame.

Thanks for taking me home. I'm sorry I bothered you last night. That was out of line. She typed then sent.

After a few minutes, he responded. *No problem.*

My mom said you're a Taurus. I hope she didn't annoy you too much. She's a little crazy.

Not at all. How are you feeling?

Like I drank way too much. I feel like death.

You threw up all over my shoes.

WHAT?? OMG are you serious? I'm so embarrassed and sorry. I don't blame you if you never want to see me again.

I needed new shoes anyway.

Do you want to do something later? Grayson held her breath as she waited for his reply.

Sorry, I have plans. I hope you feel better.

Thanks. Grayson tossed the phone onto the coffee table. This man was driving her crazy, and she barely knew anything about him. That couldn't be normal or healthy. But what did she know? She wasn't exactly an expert on men. What the hell did she expect?

She cringed. She threw up on his shoes, for crying out loud! She was probably never going to see him again. And it served her right.

Shit.

CHAPTER 21

The phone rang when Grayson was elbow deep in suds. She figured it was Luna. Still embarrassed about the last night they went out, she finished with the dishes and let the call go to voice mail. Grayson dried her hands and then tossed the towel on the counter. She reached for her phone. A smile touched her lips when she saw the missed call was from Derrick and not Luna.

She dialed his number.

"Can I see you?" Derrick's voice crossed the phone line. Her heart did that annoying flutter, which made her want to scream or kick something. He really should not have this much impact on her. It was beyond frustrating.

She'd already made plans with her sister, and should tell him no, but her brain and mouth had two different ideas. "Sure. I've got nothing going on."

"Twenty minutes?"

"I'll be waiting."

Ugh. She was so lame. Playing hard to get was obviously not her strong suit. It probably wasn't helping that she was available at his every beck and call. Next time, she would tell him no.

Yeah right...

She called her sister and canceled their plans then she spent the next twenty minutes looking out the window. The sky had darkened, and it looked like a storm was heading their way. A low rumble could be heard in the distance.

When she saw his SUV come down the road, her face broke into a goofy grin. She ran out the door, giving up any attempt at acting nonchalant. She didn't bother waiting for him to get out of the car to open her door but jumped in.

"Hey," Grayson said. She had no idea how to act around Derrick. She wanted to throw herself on him, but instead clasped her hands in front of her on her lap. It had been almost two weeks since she had seen him. Well, not counting her drunken plea for a ride home that she couldn't even recall.

"Feeling better?" he asked.

"I'm fine. It's been three days. Hangovers don't last that long."

She hadn't heard from him at all during the three days, and it made her crazy. This relationship, if that's what it could be called, was beyond confusing.

"You really should be more careful when you go out." He headed towards the highway. "When I got there, a guy was helping you outside, and his hands were wandering. You were clueless."

Grayson shuddered. The thought of some man groping her body when she was unaware made her skin crawl.

"Thanks for coming to the rescue. I don't usually drink that much. I guess I was drowning my sorrows."

"Sorrows? What kind of sorrows could be racking your pretty little head?"

He called her pretty, well her head anyway.

Answer him, you idiot, she scolded herself. What did she say? That she hadn't heard from him in over a week and was trying to forget about him? That would make her seem like a lovesick loser.

"I guess just all the stuff with Josh. I don't know how I let myself get involved with someone like him." Grayson looked out the window. "I also need to figure out what I'm going to do with myself. I can't just stay at my mom's forever. I need to finish school and maybe get a part-time job."

"Have you heard from him again?"

"He's called a few times and left messages, but I haven't returned the calls."

"Maybe you should have your mother change the house number."

"I probably should. I just hate being more of a bother to her."

"I doubt she sees you as a bother." Derrick smiled over at her. "So what are you going to school for?"

"After many attempted majors, I finally found my niche in Psychology. I want to be a counselor, but after seeing how I handle my own relationships, maybe I should reconsider. Originally, I wanted to be a geologist. I guess I don't really know what I want to do with my life anymore." She was speaking too fast, but she was a ball of nerves around him. She couldn't help herself.

Derrick laughed. "I'm sure you'll figure it out."

The conversation was making her uncomfortable, so she switched gears. "So, where are we going anyway?"

Thankfully, he let the subject go.

"I wanted to get your opinion on a piece of property I'm thinking of buying."

"Really?" Grayson sat up straighter. He actually cared what she thought? "That sounds fun. How much land?"

"Just about sixty acres. I've always wanted a place where I can shoot and have the guys over."

"Oh cool. So you're going to make a range?"

"That's the plan. But, we'll see. It won't be anything too fancy."

"Maybe I can come out and go shooting with you sometime."

He turned towards her. "You shoot?"

"What do you think?" She smiled. "Ethan is my brother. We were twelve when he started teaching us how to tear down a gun."

Derrick smiled. "That's cool."

"Do you have any brothers or sisters?"

"Nope, only child."

"That would be weird for me. I am so used to having my crazy twin and my super protective brother; I couldn't imagine it any other way." Grayson couldn't imagine a life without Luna or Ethan; they were so much a part of who she was, and they held so many of her childhood memories.

They drove for about thirty minutes chatting. Derrick left the smooth highway for a bumpy side road. Grayson was excited by the prospect that he was letting her into a private part of his world.

About a mile later, he turned down a narrow winding gravel driveway. The land was overgrown, and not that attractive. It would need a lot of work. Grayson had always been fascinated with barns as a child, and her gaze scoured the property for any sign of one.

"It's nice," Grayson said. She jumped out of the SUV and into the brush, hoping there were no snakes ready to attack.

"It could be nice. I'd have to clear a big section of the land to build the shooting range." He started walking forward.

Grayson followed, soon wishing she had worn better shoes and a rain jacket. The over growth was almost waist high, and her pants were covered with spurs. They walked up a big hill and Derrick stopped.

"I thought maybe I could build a house here someday," he said.

Grayson glanced down and could see the barn in the distance. The trees surrounding it were starting to lose their leaves. It was a good place to build. "Definitely has potential."

Derrick came up behind her and drew her roughly against him. "Yes it does," he murmured.

She leaned her head against his shoulder. His arms tightened around her. His lips lightly brushed the nape of her neck. Her whole body became tense, her breathing uneven.

"How do you have that effect on me so quickly?" she managed.

"I've wanted to touch you for days." His voice was rougher than usual.

Her knees went weak. "Really? You could have just called you know."

"We've been doing night training all week."

Ah. Well maybe he wasn't totally ignoring her, but he still could have shot her a quick text or something.

His palm was warm on her belly. Derrick's other

hand moved under her sweater and up to her breast. She was completely helpless in his arms and practically melted at his touch. Any rational thoughts flew from her head.

A moan escaped her mouth when he unbuttoned her jeans sliding his hand between her legs. He began to caress her in circular motion. He brought her to the edge, and she tried to twist around, but he held her tighter into him. His erection swelled against her jeans, sending her into sensory overload. She couldn't talk. Hell, she couldn't even think. All she could do was feel, and it was overwhelming to say the least. Within minutes, she climaxed and relaxed against him, trying to steady her breathing before turning into him. Rain softly pelted them, but they were too caught up in each other to care.

Her hands came up his hard chest in her desperation to feel the warmth from his body on her skin. Tilting her head up, her mouth urgently devoured his. His own urgency surprised and excited her at the same time. She felt utterly consumed by his kiss. When his mouth left hers, he stared down at her with an intensity that made her feel like she was the only woman in the world.

A crack of thunder startled her. Derrick grabbed her hand, pulling her behind him down the hill. They ran back to the SUV. He opened the back door, and she climbed in. "Lay back," he said hoarsely.

Grayson did and looked up as Derrick removed her shoes, and shimmied off her jeans. She wanted him so badly she was trembling. He climbed on top of her, and she parted her knees. Her hips lifted eagerly to meet him. She cried out when he entered her and wrapped her legs around his waist, pulling him closer. When her climax came it was shockingly intense. Hot waves pulsed throughout her body, and her entire body shuddered. Grayson didn't even notice the seatbelt driving into her back and easily ignored a cramp in her leg. The pleasure far surpassed any discomfort.

CHAPTER 22

On the drive back towards town, Grayson reached over and grabbed Derrick's hand. It was funny how something as simple as holding hands could feel so intimate after mind-blowing sex. He lightly rubbed his thumb back and forth across her palm. Her hand tingled at his touch.

Her phone beeped alerting her that she had missed a call. She grabbed the phone from the cup holder. What in the world? Five missed calls from her mother? That was not good. Her mom never called. Hell, she barely knew how to use her cell phone. Maybe Josh showed up again. If that was the case, she needed to know right away, so she hit send on her mom's number. The last thing she needed right now was another altercation.

"Hey, Mom. It's Grayson. You called?"

Her mom sniffed, and Grayson's body tensed.

"What's wrong mom?"

"You don't know?"

"Know what?" Grayson asked her stomach

dropping.

"Your father, Grayson, he's dead."

"What! How? Where is he?" Grayson pulled her hand away from Derrick's.

"He had a heart attack. Apparently, he's been living in Virginia all this time. His sister Michelle called. She thought we'd liked to know."

"How kind of her," Grayson said bitterly. "I'll be home soon. When's the funeral?"

"Friday."

"Okay. Thanks for letting me know," Grayson said. She clicked off her phone and closed her eyes.

She knew should feel sad, but she felt nothing. She just learned her father had died, and she had no tears to shed. Maybe she was in shock? Or perhaps she was incapable of feeling anything for the man. It made her ill knowing he had been so close to them all this time.

"Someone died?" Derrick asked concerned.

"Yup, my father," Grayson replied with no emotion in her voice.

"I'm sorry," he said as he took his eyes off the road to look at her.

"It's okay. He wasn't exactly a model father."

"Not many seem to be," Derrick said and grabbed her hand again. The warmth of his skin soothed her rattled nerves.

"My father is...was one of those men who weren't meant to be a dad. He was a merchant marine, so he was gone two months at a time and home for one month. But what he lacked in being a father he made up for by loving our mother. The kind of love you read about in books or see in a movie."

"Are they still married? Ethan's never mentioned his father."

"Yes, technically they are. They never divorced, but my father walked out on us when I was twelve, and he never looked back. That kinda shattered the childish dream of happy ever after." Grayson looked out the window off at the horizon. "He was a Vietnam vet. He never really got over the war, but it got worse as time passed. Like a mid-life crisis or something. He started drinking all the time and watching war movies obsessively. He would rant and rave about how inaccurate the movies were. My mom tried to help him, but no one could get through to him." Grayson hesitated and continued, "He left his high-paying job with no notice. He got into three accidents, all DUIs. But he always refused to admit that he had a problem." Grayson paused, not sure how much more she was willing to share.

"One day we got into a big fight. I can't even remember what it was about now. I think it was something about the laundry. Who knows. It was something so trivial I can't even remember it. My dad just got so mad at me. He went full force right at me. All I can remember were his eyes. It was like he wasn't even seeing me. They were blank, but he was full of rage. It took everyone in the house to pull him off of me. He'd never laid a hand on me until that moment," Grayson laughed bitterly. "It seems there is something about me that brings out irrational anger in men. Anyway, I guess he got sick of it all. That night he got into his car and drove away, leaving my mother nothing other than his debt. The worst thing about it was he left on Ethan's birthday and didn't even say good-bye. Ethan always blamed me for our father leaving. I think that hurt worse than the actual loss of my father in my life. Letting down Ethan is one of the worst feelings."

"That sucks, but I'm sure he realizes it wasn't your fault. You were just a kid."

"Yeah, it was just so weird. My parents were always so happy to the point it was embarrassing to be around them. They were always dancing around the kitchen. My dad was constantly brining her flowers and jewelry. When he took off, it was just very sad. I never really felt close to him, but I was sad for my mother. She used to be an artist and hasn't touched a paintbrush since the day he left. The whole situation sucked."

It was strange that she could talk to him so freely. They barely knew each other, but for some reason, she trusted Derrick. He didn't seem like the type that would judge. He just listened.

Derrick squeezed her hand, and then rested his hand on her thigh. His hand felt heavy, warm and comforting. She was glad he was there when she got the call. Her family just didn't talk about it. They tended to sweep anything uncomfortable under the rug.

"When is the funeral?"

"My mom said it's on Friday. I guess we'll probably leave tomorrow if we're going to drive."

"Call me if you need anything," Derrick said as he pulled into her driveway.

"Thanks for today. I think you should buy the land."

"I think so, too," he said. He leaned in and kissed her lightly.

Grayson got out of the SUV. She ran up the porch stairs and through the front door. Her mother was sitting in the kitchen with the lights out, drinking tea. Tea was her mom's recipe for anything that was wrong. Grayson crossed the room and went in the kitchen. She grabbed a mug and poured herself a cup and sat next to her mom. She had no idea what to say to her, or what she could do to comfort her. She should probably hug her mom, but the situation was so uncomfortable.

"Why didn't you know, Grayson?"

"I don't know, Mom. Maybe because we were no longer bonded? Perhaps I outgrew the sixth sense? It's been a long time since I've gotten a feeling like that. What about you? Shouldn't your cards or charts have told you?"

The woman in their family all seemed to have their own odd gifts. Grayson knew when someone was hurt or has passed away. Luna had dreams about alligators when something bad happened. Grams had visions and their mom had the stars and the cards. Grams said it was the magic in their Scottish blood.

"Maybe they did and I just wasn't looking, or didn't want to see it," her mom said softly.

"It's possible. So what happened?"

"I guess his hard living finally caught up with him," her mom said, wiping away a tear. "He's such a stupid bastard. I could have helped him, if he had just let me."

I reached over and patted my mom's hand.

"He loved you mom. He just had problems."

"I know. I just thought we would grow old together. It's hard to believe he's really gone. A part of me always thought he would return to us."

"I can't believe he's been so close this whole time."

"I hate him," her mom said through clenched teeth.

"You don't mean that."

"I do. We had something special, and he threw it away. For Christ's sake, he didn't even see his children graduate. He never even knew what Ethan has accomplished."

The front door opened, and Luna and Ethan came through the door. My mother stood up and threw her arms around Ethan. He was always her favorite, probably because Ethan was the spitting image of their father. She quietly sobbed into his arms.

Luna and Grayson exchanged a glance, and she knew Luna felt just as uncomfortable as she did.

CHAPTER 23

Dread washed over Grayson as they walked through the doors of the funeral home. The last time she had been to a funeral home was at her grandmother's wake. It was one of the saddest days of her life. Her grandmother had been like a second mom to her.

It still seemed surreal to her that her father was gone—dead and never to return. She wondered if he passed on to another plane of existence. She hadn't believed in life after death until her grams died, and then she desperately hoped that there was more. Grayson needed to believe there was. It was too hard to think of her Grams being gone. She occasionally still spoke to her as if she was in the same room or car as her.

Luna gripped her arm tightly, and Grayson gave her hand a light squeeze. Having her twin nearby always gave her a sense of comfort. They'd been through everything together. Grayson glanced at her sister and was surprised to see tears running down her face. Her father leaving had always affected her more. She didn't know what to say to comfort her sister, so she said nothing.

Ethan's face was stoic, but Grayson could see his eyelid twitching. She knew it was taking all his strength to keep his emotions in check. They were walking to see their father for the first time in nearly ten years. The man who abandoned them, causing their house to be repossessed. The man who left their mom a single parent, forcing her to go back to school to support them. The man that made her accept the reality that nothing was promised, that life didn't always have a happy ending, and not to take anything for granted. Grayson should feel sorrow, but all she felt was empty. And that scared her.

The place was eerily quiet. Other than the four of them and her aunt, there was just the pastor. That alone spoke volumes. Imagine living a full life and no one showing up to show their respect at your funeral. Had her father not left them, the place would have been packed. Everyone had loved him. He was one of those rare storytellers that could keep people on the edge of their seat, the life of the party, much like Luna. But he had walked away from that life. He walked away from everyone that had loved him. She would never understand what would cause a father to do that to his children or his wife.

The pastor stood up and said a few words, but Grayson didn't hear a word he said. Her eyes were focused on the coffin. Her father was lying inside... dead. It just didn't seem real. She felt like any minute her dad would jump out and say, "Just kidding!" But she knew that was not going to happen.

Their father was a Marine. Ethan and their mom were presented with a folded flag, ironic in a way. The war was what put him in an early grave, and yet it was such a beautiful gesture. Their father was proud of serving his country. She knew the flag would mean a lot to Ethan.

Her brother rose first and stood over their father's casket. He briefly leaned down and kissed him. Ethan didn't stay long as if he couldn't handle seeing their father that way. Their mom went next. She stood over him for several minutes, her shoulders slumped. Grayson wondered what was going through her mind. She couldn't imagine standing over the man she loved most her life knowing he was gone. Throw in the fact he left her high and dry, and her mother's emotions had to be all over the place. Grayson wished there was something she could do to ease her pain, but she knew it was something she would have to get through on her own.

Grayson and Luna went next. They walked closely together, hand in hand. When Grayson looked down she gasped shocked by what she saw. It was not the man she remembered. He'd always been larger than life in her eyes. Now he looked like a shriveled old man. Whatever path he took after leaving them had not been an easy one. That much was clear. It looked like his life had literally been sucked out of him. For the first time in her life, she felt sorry for him.

Luna was sobbing next to her, but Grayson still had no tears for the man. Maybe something was really wrong with her. She felt nothing.

When they left their aunt took them over to her car and opened the trunk. "Your father's possessions," she said as she stepped aside to give them a closer look. "I thought you'd like to go through them."

Curiosity pulled Grayson to the car. She wanted to know what was left of his life. Maybe she could find the answer to the question they had all be asking. Why had he left them?

There wasn't much in the trunk. Three boxes were all that was left of her father.

Grayson peeled open the first one and everyone gathered around her. She pulled out a photo album and flipped it open. It was an old album. All the pictures were in black and white. Her mother and father were dressed in all of their hippy glory. They both had long hair parted down the middle. Their mother was gorgeous and their dad had a full beard. They were laughing and making eye contact, clearly head over heels in love. Grayson just kept flipping through the pages. Near the end of the album, their mom was pregnant with Ethan. Even in black and white you could tell she was glowing. Grayson finished with the album, passed it to the others, and grabbed another.

It was strange to see their lives through a series of photographs. There was a card she had made for her father when he was gone. It was made of green construction paper and had a cut out flower glued to the front. The paper was worn. She wondered if it was from age, or from her father looking at it often. *Hurry home Daddy we miss you* was scrawled in a child's messy penmanship. The D's in Daddy were backwards.

Scalding tears started down her face, and her body shook. She couldn't believe her father had taken this stuff with him when he left. Maybe they meant more to him then he let on.

Luna pulled her in for a hug, and they stood there crying for the man they never really knew. And now they would never get the chance.

"Look at this," Ethan said as he pulled out a

newspaper clipping from the box. It was of Ethan in uniform when he got a bronze star for valor. Their father had kept tabs on them long after he left. It made her feel a little better that he hadn't totally forgotten about them. She just wished he had contacted them. Maybe they could have helped him.

Why the hell didn't he try to talk to us? Grayson thought angrily.

"He talked about you guys all the time," Aunt Michelle said. "Your father lived with demons he couldn't get past. He went for help from the VA, but they just gave him meds that he got addicted to. And he just couldn't let go of the bottle."

"Can we keep these?" Mom asked, holding a photo album to her chest. Her blue eyes glistened with tears.

"Of course. It's all yours."

Ethan grabbed the boxes and transferred them over to his truck. He never said a word. Grayson wondered what he was thinking.

"Do you want his ashes sent to you?"

My mother nodded. "Thank you. He always said he wanted his ashes to go out to sea."

Aunt Michelle took out a piece of paper and a pen from her purse. She handed it to my mom, so she could jot down her address.

"Are you staying in town for a while?" Michelle asked.

"No, we're leaving today."

Michelle's face was drawn, and her eyes looked sad. "Maybe we could go out for brunch if you'd like?"

"Sure. That would be nice." My mother said and hugged Aunt Michelle. She was the last of my father's side that was alive, and she had no children.

They went to a local diner, and Michelle tried to fill

in the blank spots of their father's absence, but there wasn't much to tell. He'd pretty much been spiraling out of control since he'd left them. He'd been in and out of rehab. But he just couldn't kick the booze. Fits of rage came and went. It was heartbreaking to hear.

Grayson's phone buzzed in her pocket. She pulled it out and was surprised to see it was from Derrick.

How are you doing?

She looked across the table. Her mom was engrossed in a conversation with Michelle.

Ok I guess. It's strange that he's really gone. But glad we got to say good-bye.

If you need anything, you know how to reach me.

Thanks. We'll be home late tonight or early tomorrow.

Grayson put the phone back in her pocket. Maybe Derrick also thought more of the relationship then he was letting on. Or maybe he was just being considerate, because he happened to be there when she got the phone call. Either way, she was glad he sent a text. She liked knowing he was thinking of her.

CHAPTER 24

Two days later, she sent Derrick a text. She wanted to feel something other than the emptiness remaining after her father's funeral.

Want to hang out?

Sure. I'm off early today want to grab lunch?

She looked down at the phone in surprise. They had never gone out to lunch before. They met up, had crazy sex, and parted ways. Maybe this was a step in moving the relationship forward.

Lunch sounds great. I'm starving.

Ok, I'll be there soon.

About twenty minutes later, Derrick pulled up on his motorcycle. She waited impatiently until he came to the door. When the doorbell rang she counted to ten and then answered it. She was trying not to appear too eager for once.

"How are you holding up?" he asked, searching her face as he crossed through the doorway. She could see the concern in his eyes.

Grayson shrugged and looked down. It was hard for her to talk about her feelings. She didn't want to remember her father lying in the casket, a shell of the man he once was. Mentally, she felt raw and exhausted. But the moment Derrick walked through the door, she once again felt alive and wanted. "Fine, I guess. It still doesn't seem real."

"It's crazy how quickly life can be taken," Derrick said quietly.

"Yep, in the blink of an eye."

"Is your mother home?" Derrick looked into the kitchen.

"No, she's at Ethan's."

He took three steps closer, closing the distance. His strong arms coiled around her, and his familiar spicy smell brought an instant stirring of arousal. He leaned forward and rested his forehand on hers. His skin felt warm, and her heart thudded against her chest. Grayson stood on her tiptoes. His lips closed over hers. He sucked her lower lip, and a soft moan escaped her. She hadn't realized how much she'd missed his touch.

Okay, maybe that was a lie. She always missed being close to him.

Grayson wrapped her hands around his neck and pulled him even closer till their bodies were pressed together. Her legs felt weak as the kiss deepened, overloading her senses. Her panties were already damp, and she was filled with anticipation.

"My room," Grayson managed to get out. Taking a step backwards, she pulled Derrick with her down the hallway. He yanked off her shirt, unclipped her bra, and tossed his shirt off before they even made it to the door.

Derrick unzipped her jeans, tugged them off, and slipped off his shoes. He then pushed his pants down and kicked them to the side. She stared at his muscular shoulders and arms. She couldn't get over how sexy this man was. Her eyes trailed downward to find he was ready and waiting. In her eyes, he was perfection.

He nudged her back onto the bed, his palm cupping her breast causing it to instantly swell. He climbed on top of her and rested on his forearms to take some of the weight off her. He lowered his mouth and traced his tongue around her nipple. Desire shot between her legs. His hand made its way to her other breast rolling the hard nipple between his fingers, making her draw in a sharp breath. Her back arched, and she dug her nails into his back, trying not to scream and wake the entire neighborhood. When she was in his arms, everything else seemed to fade away. She loved feeling his strong body pressed to hers. Reaching up, she grabbed the back of his head and brought his lips back to hers.

Every nerve ending in her body felt like a live wire.

He used his fingers to bring her to the edge, slowly moving in and out while his thumb made a circular motion around her cli, causing her back to arch uncontrollably until she cried out in pleasure. She trembled at his touch and couldn't get enough of the slow throbbing pulse inside of her.

"So soft and warm," he murmured.

Her nails dug into his back. He gazed down at her with his intense green eyes. One of his thumbs brushed the corner of her lip.

"Derrick," she groaned.

He kissed her deeply. Grayson felt like she was going out of her mind. She hadn't known such mind numbing pleasure existed until she met Derrick.

Finally, he entered her. Moaning, she met him thrust for thrust. They were frantic for each other. It seemed like every time they were together, it was more intense then the last. They went at each other until their bodies glistened with sweat. Completely satisfied, they collapsed next to each other, exhausted.

"Lunch?" Grayson rolled over and propped herself on her elbow. They lay facing each other, their bodies relaxed and content. Grayson touched his face with her fingertips, running them along his bristled jaw and outlining his lips before leaning in for a soft, lingering kiss.

Once she pulled away, Derrick replied, "I brought sandwiches." His hand rested on the curve of her waist, his fingers absently kneading her skin. His fingers drove her mad. Every little touch was intoxicating.

Her body tensed. "Sandwiches? I thought we were going out to lunch. Like on a date."

"That's against the rules. Remember?"

"I thought you were the one that said rules are made to be broken. I'd love to go on a real date with you."

Derrick didn't say anything, and she wondered what he was thinking.

"The rules were stupid," she added.

"No, they weren't. You were right. You just got out of a bad relationship. The last thing you need is to jump into another so quickly. And of course, there is the issue of your brother. I don't think he would approve."

"I don't care what Ethan thinks."

"So what are you saying Gray?"

"I don't know. I just thought we were going out for lunch. That's all."

His hand stopped moving. "Are you happy with what we have?"

"Yes. No. I don't know." Grayson moaned and rolled onto her back and stared up at the ceiling. She had never been good at explaining herself or talking about her feelings. She wanted more. She wanted to belong to him alone, and vice versa. The thought of sharing him brought out a jealousy streak she wasn't comfortable with. But she also knew it was too soon.

"I thought this was what you wanted?" His hand was now on her stomach tracing a circle. She could feel the heat start to rise between her legs again. All he had to do was touch her and she was instantly ready to go. Her breathing quickened. She wondered if he knew that his touch made it impossible for her to think.

"It is."

"Good, because I just want you to be happy. Are you happy, Gray?"

"Very." Her legs fell to the sides and Derrick's hand made its way down and his fingers teased her when she raised her hips.

"You're so mean," she said. Groaning, she squirmed under his touch.

"And you're insatiable. I don't know if I can keep up with you, but I'm sure as hell going to try."

Grayson laughed and turned over, climbing on top of him. She slid her body down between his legs and rolled his cock into her mouth, wringing a deep grunt from him. Lunch was completely forgotten. They would just devour each other instead.

Some time later, when they were completely sated, Derrick pulled his socks on and slipped into his shoes.

"Want to go to the property?" he asked.

"You got it?"

"Yep, signed the paperwork yesterday," Derrick said with a smile.

"Hell, yeah I want to go." Grayson grinned.

"Do you have your own pistol?" Derrick stood up and tugged his shirt over his head. Grayson had to stop herself from reaching out to touch his muscular chest.

Her smile faded. "I had one, but left it in Arizona."

"Tsk, tsk."

"I know, I know. I hadn't even thought of it until you mentioned it just now."

"Well, lucky for you I brought two. I'll let you use the Sig P266. I've been curious to see just how good of a teacher your big brother was."

"Maybe we can have a competition."

Derrick laughed loudly. "I don't think that would be quite fair. I've gone through more bullets in the last decade then I could count."

Grayson walked over and grabbed a sweatshirt from her closet. "I guess we'll have to see," she said, smirking.

Derrick pulled her into him and pressed one hand to the small of her back while the other wandered into her jeans.

"We'll never leave if you keep doing that."

"I've got all day," he said, pulling her even closer.

Grayson stood on her toes and gave him a quick kiss before pulling away. "Let's go before you change your mind."

Once they reached their destination, they jumped off the motorcycle, and Grayson followed Derrick to the barn. Hidden behind a stack of wood was a small safe. He pulled out a black bag and handed it to her.

Maybe this is what had been keeping him busy the last couple of weeks.

And then he slid out a couple of large metal targets in the silhouette of a person, and hefted them over his shoulder. Grayson grinned like a loon she was so beside herself. She loved target practice. It was such a high.

They walked down a narrow path surrounded by shrubs and came out into a small clearing.

"Is this the first time you've been out to shoot?" Grayson asked.

"Yep. It's going to take a while to get it set up nicely, but this should do for today. I've been bringing some of my gear out here and starting to clean up the mess."

Derrick set up the targets and handed Grayson ear protection.

"Do you want me to go over the basics with you?" Derrick asked as he filled the cartridge with bullets. Grayson gave him a look and grabbed an empty casing and helped out.

Derrick shook his head and smiled. "Just when I thought you couldn't get any sexier."

"Is that so?" Grayson took a step forward, and Derrick put up his hand.

"Don't try to distract me. I'm starting to think I might actually have some competition."

"You should know better than to underestimate your opponent. I think we need to put a wager on the table."

"So what are the stakes of this so-called wager of yours?"

"If I win, you have to take me to the movies."

Derrick raised an eyebrow. "And if I win?"

"That's up to you," Grayson said as she hefted the familiar weight of the gun. She slammed the cartridge into the bottom and pulled back the slide putting a round in the chamber.

"I'll have to think it over," Derrick said as he walked out to the target and counted paces back toward her. "We'll start at nine meters."

"Okay," Grayson said as she rolled her eyes. She was actually a little nervous, because it had been a while since she'd gone shooting. And her brother always reminded her it was a perishable skill.

"Two to the chest one to the head," Derrick said.

Grayson nodded, and put on her ear and eye protection before walking up to the line Derrick had etched on the ground. She placed her right foot forward and leaned her body in, holding her arms tight. Blocking everything around her the way her brother drilled into her head, she lined up the sites and squeezed the trigger in rapid succession. She loved the ping of the bullet hitting the metal. It made her feel powerful and untouchable. Of course, that wasn't really true. She'd been able to shoot just as well when she was with Josh and look how that turned out.

Derrick whistled under his breath. "Okay, so you were telling the truth. Obviously, we're going to have to up the ante."

Grayson watched Derrick. His hands were at his sides and the gun in his holder. When the buzzer went off, he grabbed the gun, emptied the bullets, dropped the magazine and replaced it with another in the blink of an eye. Grayson was impressed and more than a little turned on.

"I'm going to get some paper targets," Derrick uttered as he turned and hurried back to the barn.

They spent the next couple of hours going through drills and competitions. Derrick always won, but it was the most fun Grayson could remember having in a long time. She felt relaxed around him. There was no need for any false pretense. She could be herself.

After they packed up, Derrick grabbed her around the waist. "Not bad for a girl," he said playfully.

"You're not sexist are you?"

"Of course not. I'm just teasing. Anyone can learn to shoot accurately with enough time and practice."

"This was fun. Can we do it again—soon?"

"Yeah. I'd like that."

"So what are you going to claim for your victory?"

"I thought that was obvious." He pulled her tighter to him. As always her pulse went into overdrive.

Grayson stared up at him innocently, her eyes wide.

"Not a clue," she said, secretly hoping that his claim was something sexual.

Derrick took the gun out of her hand, removed the cartridge and made sure it was clear before he set it on the table.

He unzipped her sweatshirt and pulled off one sleeve and then the other.

"What if someone comes out here?" Grayson said, looking around.

"Then I guess they'll get an eye full," he said with a sexy grin.

"It's really cold out."

"You don't look very cold to me," Derrick said, his voice barely above a whisper. He framed her face with his warm hands, and her arms slipped under his shirt. It was preposterous the way she trusted him blindly. Any caution was thrown to the wind when he was around.

"Is this normal?" she asked in a hushed voice.

"Is what normal?"

"This. Us."

His lips trailed up her throat. He drew her earlobe gently between his teeth. "I guess that depends on what your definition of normal is."

CHAPTER 25

Time was passing quickly. She had been involved with Derrick for over three months. Three months of crazy hot and heavy sex. Where had the time gone? Fall had turned into winter, and there was a light dusting of snow on the ground. She picked up her phone and gave him a call.

"Hey do you want to hang out tonight?"

"Sorry, I can't."

"Big plans?" She was starting to think he was awful busy for a single man. Perhaps he had a serious girlfriend or hell maybe he was married.

No, Heather would have known if he was married. She didn't even care if he did — or so she liked to tell herself. She'd just like to know about it. They'd agreed they were not exclusive. Hell, they weren't even dating. They were sexual partners and nothing more. What scared her was the fact that the thought of being with anyone else had completely lost its appeal.

Luna was getting fed up with her, because she didn't join her in her man chasing anymore. Grayson had gone home alone every time they went out. She wasn't even tempted. All she wanted was Derrick. Her days seemed to revolve around waiting on a text or a phone call from him, which didn't come nearly as often as she would like. And she knew it was not in any way healthy to become this obsessive, but she couldn't seem to stop herself and let him go.

"No big plans, really just hanging out with the guys."

"Okay, well have fun."

"What about you, what are you going to do?"

"No idea. Probably just stay home and watch a movie or read I guess."

"Okay cool. Hey, I got to go, but I'll call you tomorrow."

Grayson hung up the phone and dropped her head in her hands. She was way more into Derrick then she should be. He was going to crush her heart, she knew it, but she still couldn't stop quietly obsessing over him.

Their meetings were sporadic at best. Sometimes they would see each other three days in a row, and others more than a week would pass. She was ready to pull out her hair she was so confused by his actions and her emotions. She kept telling herself she should end their sordid relationship, but anytime she went to tell him they should stop he would do or say something that made it impossible. She felt like she needed rehab. She was an addict, and no one else but Derrick could feed her addiction. She was disgusted with herself.

Her phone rang, and her heart dropped. Maybe he changed his mind. Luna's name flashed across the screen.

"Oh, it's you."

"Is that any way to treat your sister? Who were you expecting?"

"No one, I'm just tired, sorry."

"Sure. Anyways, want to go out? I heard there is a new band playing."

Grayson glanced around the kitchen. She might as well go out. It was either that or another night home alone with the cats. Her mother worked the night shift at the hospital so she was alone at night. She couldn't sit around twiddling her thumbs waiting on Derrick.

What was wrong with her? She left one bad relationship and was starting to cling to a virtually nonexistent one with someone who only thought of her as an occasional fuck buddy. He was by her new standards perfect, and yet she was miserable.

"Fine, but let's go back to that pub," she said thinking that maybe she would run into Derrick there.

"Um, okay," Luna said, "but there are no bands there."

"I know. It's quieter at the pub, and we haven't been there in a while."

"Okay. Come pick me up. I don't feel like driving, and your Jeep is better in the snow."

"I'll be there in an hour," Grayson said, and hung up the phone so fast that Luna couldn't even say bye.

Grayson immediately went to throw on some clothes. She pulled out a green long-sleeve shirt. As she looked in the mirror to check herself out, all she could focus on was the green color of her shirt; it reminded her of Derrick's eyes.

Could I be anymore pathetic? Why does life have to be so damn confusing?

She knew why. She was falling in love with Derrick. The thought alone pissed her off. It had been almost a week since the last time she saw him. He'd brought her to a hotel, yet again. Grayson had asked him if he was going to stay the night in the hotel, if so she'd come back and see him.

When he said no, a red flag instantly rose. If he was living with a buddy with a kid like he claimed, he should jump at the chance of being on his own. She had a sinking feeling it had more to do with the fact that he had someone to go home to. She thought about following him after he left the hotel, but she wasn't that crazy.

Thank god. Screw him. Grayson thought. Tonight she was going home with someone else.

Grayson took extra care with her appearance that evening, which Luna certainly approved of. An hour later, she pulled up to her sister's house. Luna climbed into the passenger seat.

"Don't you ever get sick of this?" Grayson asked.

"Sick of what, little sister? Sick of having wild sex, and not having a care in the world about it? No way in hell."

Grayson sighed. There was no reasoning with her sister.

"Grayson, we're just doing what men have been doing since the beginning of time. Taking what we want, and enjoying it until the next best thing comes along. I'd say it's about time the tables were turned."

"What's next? Are we going to burn our bras in the front yard?" Grayson said wryly.

"Nah. Bras are a needed accessory."

"Do you think you'll ever settle down?" Grayson turned on the blinker and eased onto the highway.

"Who knows. At this point I haven't met anyone that is worthy of all my time," Luna said, shrugging.

Grayson smiled.

"Besides, I don't think monogamy is natural."

"Ever?" Grayson asked.

"Ever. Even if I get serious with someone, it will be an open relationship."

"I don't know, I like the thought of having one partner for life, just not anytime soon. Not after the disaster of a relationship I had with Joshua."

They talked all the way to the bar.

When they arrived, Grayson scanned the bar looking for someone to take her mind off Derrick, even if it was only for a few hours. It didn't take long for her to single someone out. A tall, dark-haired man leaned against the bar talking to his buddies. He had an easy confidence about him that she found sexy. Feeling bold, she walked up between him and his friend and ordered two drinks for her and Luna.

Grayson turned and smiled at him.

He gave her an once-over and smiled in approval. "What's your name?" He asked, his voice was deep and sent a small thrill through her.

"Grayson," she said. She didn't feel the need to give him a false name.

"I'm Christopher and this is my buddy Brody."

Grayson turned to take in his friend. He was well built blond and had shaggy hair. He looked like a surfer. Luna would approve.

"Why don't you guys come sit with me and my sister? She pointed at Luna.

"Twins? That's funny," Christopher laughed.

"What's so funny about it?" She braced herself for another annoying joke that would just piss her off.

"I have a twin brother."

"Really? Well that is interesting."

He flipped through images on his phone and showed her his clone. She looked at the image and then back at Christopher. "Your brother is hot."

He rolled his eyes with a grin. "A sense of humor and good looks? It must be my lucky day."

"Maybe it is," Grayson said, grinning back at him. She actually enjoyed the flirty banter. Maybe tonight was just what she needed. Escape from reality.

The bartender put the drinks on the bar, and Brody paid grabbing Luna's drink. Grayson took a sip from her drink. The whiskey tasted smooth and warm going down, just how she liked it. They headed over to the table.

Luna and Brody soon took off to play a game of pool. Her sister seemed happy with her new companion. Not that it was hard to make her happy. Luna's taste was vast and varied. Grayson watched her leave and wondered if her sister would ever find someone that would make her want to settle down.

An hour later she was surprised to find she actually enjoyed Christopher's company. He was intelligent, funny and not bad to look at. Just what she needed to get her mind off the one man she couldn't really have.

Relaxing and enjoying herself with Christopher, Grayson looked up, and her stomach fell.

You have got to be kidding me. Derrick walked in with the same blonde girl by his side. *Just hanging out with the guys, my ass!*

He noticed her, and then his gaze shifted to Christopher, he kept his face neutral the entire time. She had been hoping he would come tonight, but wasn't expecting a girl to be glued to his freaking side. Her blood boiled. She knew it!

Damn him. She blinked back tears and reached up

to trail her finger down the side of her companions face. He grabbed her hand and kissed her fingertips.

Without thinking she grabbed the back of his head and pulled him towards her. He pulled back and looked at her questionably and she bit the corner of her lip.

"Jesus, Grayson," he whispered before his lips crashed down on hers. She could feel Derrick's eyes on hers, and she intensified the kiss.

She pulled away and took a long swig off her drink, and grabbed her coat. "Let's get out of here," she said with urgency in her voice.

"You don't have to ask me twice," Christopher said. He stood up and followed her out.

Grayson glanced back, and Derrick's eyes were on her. He didn't look happy at all.

Screw him.

It gave her a small amount of pleasure to see his still face finally show some trace of emotion. He couldn't even take her out to lunch, and yet this dishwater blonde chick was always by his side. He could go to hell for all she cared.

She had given him the opportunity to be with her tonight. Obviously, his other plans were more important.

Yup. He can go to hell for all I care.

Once outside, Christopher pressed her back against the cold brick building. Even after being in a bar, he smelled good. That in itself is quite an accomplishment. Usually people end up smelling like an ashtray. He smelled like the woods on a rainy day. He was very tall and broader than she first realized. His eyes were light brown and reminded her of caramel. His hand went behind her hair and his lips met hers gently at first and then with more urgency. She could hear people walking by, but she didn't care. She let herself get lost in the kiss. Between the alcohol and her anger at Derrick, it was easy to do.

Grayson pulled away to catch her breath. He was an incredible kisser, which made her wonder if his skills transferred into other areas. Soon she would find out.

They walked across the parking lot and down the main street. His hotel was to the left. His arm draped across her shoulders, and she welcomed the warmth on the cold evening. Once inside the elevator Christopher couldn't keep his hands off her. She thought of Derrick with the girl, and any sense of guilt washed away.

Two can play this game.

CHAPTER 26

Rolling over Grayson groaned inwardly. She hadn't meant to fall asleep with—what was his name? She thought about it for a moment. Christopher. What a mess she was.

His warm brown eyes opened. "Morning," he said with a sleepy smile on his face.

"I should go," Grayson replied and threw the blankets off her, but Christopher pulled her back.

"Not yet. You can't leave until I feed you. You don't want me to feel like I've been used do you?"

Grayson fell back into the bed. She was hungry. Derrick crossed her mind, but she pushed him out of her mind. If anything it made her focus more on Christopher. It turned her on knowing he had been pissed last night. Maybe it was just what he needed to decide if he wanted her to himself or not.

"Besides, it's supposed to be the guy slipping out in the morning not the female," Christopher said. He tossed his long leg over hers and pulled her closer. His lips grazed her ear.

Her body relaxed into his. Maybe food could wait.

He was very sweet.

Christopher rolled her on top of him. She giggled, and her hair fell all around her onto his chest.

"You're even sexier in the morning," he whispered. His warm breath tickled her neck. "How is that possible?"

Grayson's eyes met his and smiled. "Hmm, I don't know. Lack of booze maybe?"

"I'm pretty sure it's usually the opposite," Christopher said as his large, warm hands ran up and down her bare back.

Leaning down, she lightly bit his lip, causing him to groan. She worked her way down his chest. His hands knotted in her hair, she trailed her tongue up the length of his hard cock and smiled up at him.

"You are so fucking hot."

Grayson flicked her tongue across the tip of him before wrapping her lips completely around him.

After a few minutes of teasing him Grayson made her way back up. Christopher grabbed a condom off the nightstand. Grayson rolled it over his hard cock, and then slowly slid onto him.

Christopher pushed himself up, pulling her with him to sit against the headboard, and his tongue flicked her nipple. She arched her back as his warm mouth covered her breast, and his hands griped her ass as she slowly ground her hips into his. God she loved se!. She loved how it cleared her mind when she gave into the sensations of passion. There was too much pleasure available in this world to be miserable.

She was surprised how gentle Christopher had been. As ridiculous as it sounded, it felt like he made love to her instead of fucking her. It was a nice change of pace. With Derrick, everything was so intense and passionate. She always felt filled with greed with Derrick, like she couldn't get enough.

Slow and sweet was a nice change.

A while later, they lay in silence, sated and satisfied.

"Room service?"

Grayson stretched her arms. "Sure. I don't feel like moving," she said lazily.

"I should tell you something," Christopher said, clearing his throat.

"Stop right there," Grayson said as she tugged the sheet and tucked it under her chin. "We don't have to go any further than a one-night stand. No spilling of secrets. I really don't care or want to hear whatever you feel the need to tell me."

"I'm married," he spit out.

Married? Well, she really shouldn't be surprised. *Guess I can add home wrecker to my list of sins.* She was convinced she was going to hell.

"That's okay," she replied. "I'm emotionally unavailable anyway."

"You're not freaked out?"

"Why should I be? I don't even know you, and I'll probably never see you again," Grayson said, shrugging it off.

"That's the thing. I want to see you again," he said, meeting her gaze.

"You're not even from here." She looked at him, puzzled.

"Yeah, but I travel—a lot. I could fly you out to see me."

"So, what you want me to do is be the other woman? Have a scandalous affair with you?" Grayson said then laughed.

"Just think it over. I get lonely and would love the

company. I'm going to New York after here, and then California."

"What about your wife?"

"I love her," he said simply.

"Obviously," Grayson said sarcastically.

"I do. We've just grown apart, and to say our sex life is lacking would be an understatement. But to be clear I have no intention of leaving her, ever."

The thought of traveling was somewhat appealing. Christopher was sweet and sexy, but he was married.

"I don't think so," Grayson replied and tossed off the covers. "Let's order. I'm starving." She pulled on her underwear.

Chris nodded. "I'm not giving up that easily."

"Do you always hook up when you're out of town?"

He threw his head back and laughed. "No. It's not every day a young woman asks me to take her home."

Heat rose to her face. She was the one to pursue him. "I didn't know you were married. You're not wearing a ring."

He glanced down at his hand. "I don't wear a ring when I work."

"Going to a bar is work?" Grayson looked at him like, *yeah, right buddy.*

"I mean when I'm gone, period. I just leave my ring at home."

"Your wife doesn't mind?"

"No, in my line of work most guys don't wear rings," he shrugged.

"What's your line of work?"

"It would bore you."

"I doubt it," Grayson told him as she tilted her head to look at him closer.

The doorbell rang, and room service was delivered.

They ate and chatted like old friends. She was surprised to find she had connected with him so quickly. Maybe it was because nothing would come from their hook up, or maybe it was just that he seemed really interested in her.

"So why are you emotionally unavailable?" Christopher asked as he buttered his toast. "I'm sure there is a sad story involved."

"I fell for a jackass, and it ended badly. Then I fell for a guy who isn't as into me as I am him."

"Present tense huh? Sorry, but I find that hard to believe he's not that into you."

Grayson reached for a napkin. "It's complicated," she said while mentally slapping herself in the face for bringing up Derrick.

"Isn't it always? Do you always tear apart napkins when you're uncomfortable?"

She looked down at the table and saw she had torn the poor napkin to shreds and wasn't even aware of it. "Actually, he walked into the bar last night with another woman."

"Ah, it all makes sense now! Revenge sex. That hurts a little," he said as he clutched his chest.

"I wouldn't call it that. I would have gone home with you, even if he hadn't walked in. I think."

"Right place. Right time." Christopher's lip quirked up. "I'd thank him if I could. For the record, he's a fool."

"I think I'm the fool. Let's talk about something else."

They spent the next hour asking each other questions, and getting to know the other better. It was nice. She learned more about this guy in one night then she had about Derrick in three months. How was that possible?

When she got up to leave, Grayson grabbed the pen off the desk and scribbled her email address. "We'll keep in touch, but no promises."

He smiled and pulled her into his chest. He pressed his lips to hers and kissed her deeply. When he finally pulled away they were both slightly breathless. "Just in case I don't see you again," he said giving her a charming wink and smile.

She nodded and walked out the door without saying anything.

Well, that had been interesting. She touched her lips and looked back at the door. She was surprised by how much she enjoyed Christopher's company, but it wasn't like how it was with Derrick. With Derrick, it was exciting and with Chris, it had been comfortable.

What the hell was she thinking? He was a married man! Maybe there wouldn't be any harm in staying friends with him. The male companionship was nice. The sex was more than ok, and at least he was honest with her about what he wanted.

CHAPTER 27

Grayson pulled herself into the Jeep. She plugged in her phone and drummed her fingers on the steering wheel, waiting for it to turn on. She had a couple of missed calls from Luna and a text from Derrick. Even though she was pissed at him, her heart still sped up, seeing he'd messaged her. She once again thought that she should probably put an end to this crazy relationship. The up and down was driving her absolutely bonkers.

Enjoy yourself?

Grayson stared at his message and debated on responding. Of course, she lacked any sense of self-control, and it gave her a small sense of pleasure to get under his skin.

Immensely. You?

Not really.

Her fingers flew across the keyboard. *That's too bad. Perhaps you picked the wrong date?* She was acting like a child, and she knew it, but she didn't care.

Maybe I did. I want to see you.

I'm busy. Grayson stared down at the phone nervously and waited for his reply, but was met with silence. A few moments later her phone buzzed. Relief wash over her.

How about tonight?

The thought of having sex with two different guys on the same day made her feel more than a little gross. *I have plans tonight with Luna. How about tomorrow?*

Ok. Around 10am?

Sure. He must really be anxious to see her. They usually saw each other in the afternoon or evening.

Lost in her thoughts, Grayson made her way to her mother's. She couldn't wait to crawl back in bed.

The next morning, Grayson dropped into the passenger seat of Derrick's SUV. He stared at her without saying a word. His face was expressionless as usual, which made her want to scream or throw something at him. She wondered if it was hard for him to constantly keep his emotions hidden, or if it just came naturally to him. Either way it pissed her off.

She might as well get it out in the open, she was sick of all the mind games they were playing. "So that's your girlfriend?"

"I told you. She's not my girlfriend."

"Sure looks that way to me," she said as she propped her feet up on the dashboard.

"Who was the knucklehead you were with last night?"

"He's not a knucklehead, and his name is Christopher. He happens to be very nice."

"First time you've been with him?" Derrick asked

glancing over at her. "Or is this someone you knew already?"

"Well, technically it was three times. Twice last night and once early in the morning before breakfast." She just had to get that dig in. Especially since Derrick had never stayed the night with her.

His hands tightened on the steering wheel. She could see his knuckles whiten. Her lips twitched trying to hide her satisfied smile.

"And where did he fall on your sliding scale?"

"I don't think that's any of your business."

"I guess you're right."

Grayson tilted her head and took in his strong profile. "Does it bother you?"

He didn't say anything for a minute. He appeared to be in deep thought. "Free will, so it doesn't matter if it bothers me or not. You're grown woman. You can do what you want," he answered finally, expressionless.

"That's not an answer."

"Well, that's all you're going to get."

"What if I said I wanted you? And only you," she asked.

"I thought you didn't want a relationship? No strings. No dating. No falling in love, remember?"

"Maybe I changed my mind. I don't like seeing you with someone else. It sort of pisses me off."

"Too bad," he said.

Grayson's heart sank.

"I'm leaving for three months next week," he continued. "Not the best time to start a relationship. And no offense, but I have a hard time believing you'd wait for me to come back."

"And why is that? Don't you trust me?"

Derrick stayed silent and refused to look her way.

"You don't trust me, because of what your ex did, not because of anything I've done. And you know what? That's cool. I get it. I guess we all have our baggage."

"That's not the reason." His troubled eyes met hers, and she felt her heart rate speed up. She wasn't sure if she should press the issue, but she couldn't help herself. She saw a window and had to take it.

"Would you ditch the blonde?"

"I already told you we're not dating."

Grayson rolled her eyes and dropped her head back against the seat.

"You also told me you were going out with the guys."

"I was. They arrived after you left."

"I see." Clearly, she wasn't going to get what she wanted out of this conversation, and honestly she wasn't even sure if she really wanted an actual relationship anyway. Like he said he was leaving for three months and would be gone often with his job. She was somewhat enjoying her newfound freedom, and the opportunity to explore different people. Maybe she would take Christopher up on his offer and see some new places.

No she wouldn't. He was married, for crying out loud!

"Fine." Grayson sighed and looked out the window.

"Fine, what?"

"We'll just keep this crazy mind game we have going on. I can't seem to walk away from you even though every bone in my body believes you are lying about the girl. I think she's your girlfriend, if not more."

Derrick tapped the steering wheel. "I wasn't going to see you again after last night."

"Oh really, is that right? You walk in the bar with

another girl and you're going to stop seeing me? That makes a lot of sense." He was seriously starting to piss her off.

"Touché. As you can see I wasn't able to walk away either."

"Well, isn't this an interesting predicament we've gotten ourselves into."

"That's one way to look at it."

They pulled into yet another hotel. By now, they visited almost all the hotels in the area. She thought it was absurd he spent the money for just a couple of hours.

"Stay the night with me," she said nervously.

He took a deep breath, but didn't say anything.

"I take that as a no? Maybe you should just take me home."

"I didn't say no. Why don't I just say we'll see?"

"I guess we will," Grayson mumbled and jumped out of the SUV.

Going to hotels was starting to make Grayson feel dirty. It had once been exciting, but now she felt like he was ashamed to be seen in public with her. Which was absurd, since she's the one that made the no dating rule to begin with. Part of her wished she could go back to the day they first met and let the relationship take its normal course instead of setting stupid guidelines, but there was no rewind button on life.

Derrick was even more aggressive than usual. He roughly pushed her legs a part and shoved two fingers into her while his tongue flicked her clit.

"Did Christopher do this?"

She squirmed beneath his touch. Grayson shook

her head yes. She really wanted to piss him off. She knew it wasn't nice, but she couldn't help herself. Her reply just seemed to turn him on even more. Her hands gripped his head, and her body shuddered when an orgasm ripped through her body in waves. God he was incredible!

"Turn over."

Grayson lay still and smiled up at him.

"Turn over, Gray." His green eyes bore into hers daring her not to comply.

She turned on her hands and knees, but he pushed her flat onto the bed and shoved his cock deep into her. "Did he do this?"

Gasping, and unable to speak, she just shook her head no. She couldn't even move with his weight on her. He grabbed her hair and pulled her head back. "Did he fuck you good?"

Grayson groaned and mumbled, "no." Her pussy was dripping wet. She should have been freaked out by the questions, but it made her body tingle all over. Excitement prickled the back of her neck.

"What?"

"I said no," Grayson groaned as he slammed into her.

"Don't lie to me," he growled. "You enjoyed it didn't you?" He continued to pound away at her and she nodded her head yes. He let go of her hair and whispered, "That wasn't so hard was it?"

He grabbed her waist and pulled her back up onto her hands and knees. One of his calloused hands caressed her throat. "Are you going to see him again?"

Suddenly, all she could think about was Joshua's hands wrapped around her throat. She tensed up, and turned to look at him as if reminding herself he

was not Josh. Her eyes must have given away her fear.

"Gray? Are you ok?"

She blinked back tears, "Yes, I'm fine. Sorry, I'm just being stupid."

Derrick pulled out and she rolled over.

"I would never hurt you. You know that right?" He ran his fingers along her collarbone.

"I know you wouldn't." And she really did know that. He would never intentionally physically hurt her. She wasn't sure why she knew that or felt that way, but she believed that one hundred percent.

"Are you sure? If you think I'm too aggressive, I'll ratchet it back. I didn't mean to scare you."

"No, I like it. I love it really. I guess your hand on my throat just kind of freaked me out in that moment. Seriously, it's not you. It's just a bad movie that plays in my head sometimes."

"Fucking bastard. I should have done more damage to him when I had the chance."

"I think he got the picture." Grayson ran her hand up the length of his cock, and he quickly grew hard again. She wasn't going to let a memory of Josh ruin her time with Derrick. She gripped him tightly working him with her hand. "I don't know if I'll see Christopher again." She whispered. "He wants me to though."

"Will you?" Derrick settled himself between her legs.

"Yes," she whispered. Why she said yes she wasn't sure? Did she really plan on seeing him again? Or was she just trying to get under his skin?

"What if I said I didn't want you to?" He slowly eased himself in and out of her.

"I wouldn't see him again," she said breathlessly. Her heart raced. His face was only inches away. He grasped her wrists firmly and then slowly moved his hands down her arms sending a shiver through her body.

"Do you mean that?" His eyes searched hers as he slid deeper into her, and she wrapped her legs around his waist and pulled him closer.

"Yes. I only want you."

His lips came crushing down on hers. He kissed her like he needed her as much as he needed air to breath. Their pace became frantic moving fast and hard. He plunged deep within her as if he intended to penetrate her soul. A low growl came out of his mouth, and his body shuddered as he climaxed inside of her.

A few minutes later, when he had recovered, he pulled her against him.

"Did you mean what you said?" Grayson laid her head on his chest and listened to the rhythm of his heartbeat.

"What?"

"You don't want me to see Christopher again?"

"I didn't say that," he said as he ran his hand through her hair.

"You implied it."

"Gray, I told you. You can see and do whatever you want. I'm not going to ask you not to. It wouldn't be fair."

"Why not? Is it because you have a girlfriend?"

"I'm not getting into that again with you. It's because I'm leaving and it's not the right time to start a relationship."

"If she's not your girlfriend, then why is she always with you?"

"She's a friend. I've known her for years, and she's on our adventure racing team."

Grayson thought about it, and it seemed plausible.

"I'd wait for you," Grayson said, feeling completely exposed.

"I'm not going to ask you to wait. That would be selfish."

"What if I said I like when you're selfish with me? What if I said I wanted to belong to you and no one else?"

"Don't say that." His hand moved to her thigh, and she could feel his renewed arousal pressed against her.

"I mean it. I know it's crazy, but I want this. I want you."

He shook his head. "Sorry Gray, it's not going to happen."

Coldness passed through her body. She knew he wanted her as much as she wanted him. She could feel it when he touched her. Sense it when he looked at her. Why wouldn't he admit it? Probably, because of the damn blonde chick.

Bitch.

"I'm going to wait for you."

"Like I said. Free will."

"Stay the night with me."

"Not tonight, maybe another time."

Anger rose up into her chest. She was willing to give him everything, and he couldn't even spend one night with her.

"Well then I guess I should go," Grayson said sharply and jerked away from him, but he pulled her back. Just like he always did—pushed her away and pulled her back. His lips found hers, and his tongue ran along the top of her lip causing a sigh to escape.

She pulled away. "Derrick. I think I'm falling..."

"Shh, don't say it Gray. You can't take it back once the words are out. Let's see where things are when I get back. You'll probably have moved on by then."

"I won't."

"You don't know that." His lips met hers. He kissed her softly and rolled her onto him. This time he was very sweet and gentle. Being with him was like being on a crazy roller coaster: Up and down and scary as hell.

CHAPTER 20

Today was the last time she would see Derrick for three months. Sadness washed over her. The last week they spent almost every day together except on the weekend. They'd even gone shooting again on his property, which was a lot of fun. Grayson went out with her sister on Saturday, but didn't go home with anyone. She just *couldn't* go home with anyone. Christopher had emailed inviting her to join him on a weekend getaway, but she ignored the email. All she could think about was wanting to be with Derrick.

She pulled her Jeep into the parking lot of the hotel. It was the same place they had sex for the first time. It was sort of sweet, well more bittersweet, that he picked the place they had first had sex to say good-bye. Grayson reached down and grabbed the paper bag under the passenger seat, and pulled the Thor's hammer pendant out of it. It was quite beautiful with the intricate knot work. She came across it while browsing a local New Age store looking for crystals. Derrick reminded her of a Viking so she thought the gift was fitting. Her brother always said they were going overseas to bring down the thunder whenever he got deployed. So the hammer made her smile. Hopefully, he would like it.

Today she was going to tell Derrick that she had unwillingly fallen in love with him, and wanted to wait for him to return. And she wasn't going to take no for an answer. He would just have to deal with it.

Where the hell was he? She looked into the review mirror. He was over thirty minutes late, and he was always punctual—if not early.

Are you coming? She texted him at last.

I got caught up with work. It's crazy here before we head out.

A text would have been nice. I've been sitting in the parking lot for almost an hour.

Go home. I don't think I'll be out of here for a while.

So I'm not going to see you before you leave?

Doesn't look like it.

Lovely, thanks.

I'll be sure to keep in touch with you through emails and Skype.

When are you leaving?

Really early in the morning.

Of course you are.

What does that mean?

You have to spend your last evening with someone else. Grayson hesitated and then hit send. Even though she dreaded his reply she had to get it off her chest.

I gotta go. See you in three months.

That's it? Grayson stared down at the phone and was surprised to feel tears well up in her eyes. She had been looking forward to spending one more day with him before he left. Obviously, she wasn't worth the effort. God she was an idiot!

Take care of yourself.

You don't have to worry about me. I'll be just fine. Grayson hit send and threw the phone into the cup holder with a lot more force than usual.

Somehow she managed to get through the motions of the rest of her day. Grayson cleaned the house, went for a run, showered and then decided to go to the bookstore. She was trying not to feel sorry for herself, but it bothered her more than she'd liked to admit. Her heart ached, and her head throbbed. She had to continuously keep herself in check so she didn't cry. If there was one thing that always calmed her it was the smell of books and coffee.

She browsed the new releases and then made her way to the cafe. When she looked up, she dropped the book in her hand with a loud clunk. Derrick was sitting at the table talking to the blonde.

You have to be fucking kidding me!

The room suddenly became hot, making it hard for her to breathe. She was frozen, not knowing what to do or say. She watched them for several minutes before he noticed her. They were sitting too close to be just friends, and the girl was also very interested in whatever was coming out of his mouth. She felt like she was breaking apart on the inside.

Their eyes met, and Derrick did something that nearly brought her to her knees—he looked away.

For a moment, she forgot to breathe. She wanted to go say hello just to make him uncomfortable, and watch him squirm. Her throat was too tight for her to get any words out. The last thing she needed was to confront Derrick and give the blonde the pleasure of hearing her voice crack.

So much for the bookstore calming her. Grayson practically ran out the front door.

Once in her Jeep with shaky hands she sent Derrick a text.

I guess I see where I rate on your scale.

She waited, but there was no return text. She threw her phone out of frustration, and it hit the bag with the pendant inside of it. How could she have been so naive to believe him? What really bothered her was the fact that he lied about the girl. They had agreed they were not exclusive, and she had told him when she went off with someone else. And yet Derrick kept insisting there was nothing going on with the blonde. She dropped her head back against the seat and closed her eyes. Anger and disappointment filled her body. What she should do is go back in there and throw the gift at him, and just walk away confidently.

Why didn't I listen to my damn sister-in-law? That's what I get for falling in love with a man who didn't feel the same. Isn't life grand?

She wished she could forget her time spent with Derrick. Instead, she seemed to be able to think of nothing else but those hours spent with the man she fell in love with. Anger and rage churned in her stomach.

Grayson pushed the door open and walked up and down the rows of cars in the parking lot until she found Derrick's black Chevy. The pewter pendant felt heavy in her hand. She draped it over the driver's side mirror and walked away. What was intended as a see-you-soon gift was now a good-bye present. He might not even notice it when he got in the car, and it would end up on the highway somewhere.

Whatever. It's probably better off that way.

CHAPTER 29

A week later, Grayson was online checking out colleges when her messenger chimed. It was Derrick. She was disgusted with herself that her heart hammered against her chest when his name popped up. Why the hell did her body respond like this? Too bad there wasn't some kind of off switch.

Sorry about the bookstore. His message said.

Are you? You could have fooled me.

How have you been?

I'm fine. What did you think I would fall apart after you left? Don't give yourself too much credit.

I wasn't thinking that at all. Just asking how you're doing.

A week is a long time to let pass before contacting me.

It always takes a while to get Internet connection when we get over here. I figured you knew that from Ethan.

She did know that was true, but had forgotten about it in her fury. Surely, he could have sent her a text before he left. So he wasn't off the hook. And she wasn't stupid enough to get pulled back into his web of lies. She was done, depleted, and worn out.

You could have sent me a text that evening or the morning you were leaving.

You're right I could have. I should have.

It doesn't matter.

Sorry you feel that way.

Seriously? You have a lot of nerve.

Gray, you have gone home with several men since we've been together.

I didn't hide it from you. I didn't lie about it. I've gone home with two men, not several. And both times I did, it was because I was pissed at you, she replied.

And?

And nothing.

How do I know you're telling the truth? We never agreed to give a tally just to use protection. Correct? He challenged.

You're right. Neither of us is blameless, but you should have told me the truth.

If you don't want to chat I won't contact you again.

I do want to talk to you. I'm just confused, and I guess hurt. Why wouldn't her brain co-operate with her hands?

Grayson, we agreed this was casual.

I know. I'm a fool. Just so you know after the bookstore incident, I can't wait for you. I have too much self-respect for that.

I didn't expect you to.

I would have waited….

Maybe. I guess we'll never know.

Guess not. In a way, I'm glad I saw you. She told him.

Oh?

Yeah, I would have been pissed if I waited around for three months. I guess I either have to be happy with what we have or move on. I'm leaning towards moving on.

That's up to you.

Obviously.

Let's just see what happens when I get back. Ok?

She blew out a breath. *Ok.*

Later that evening she went out with Luna and finally filled her in on Derrick. She had kept it a secret, but Luna wasn't stupid. She knew something had been going on.

"Well that sucks," Luna said thoughtfully. Grayson was surprised her sister didn't lecture her.

"I asked for it."

"Yeah maybe, but why would he pick someone else over you? I personally take insult to that as someone who looks exactly like you."

Grayson shrugged and tried not to let the tears start flowing. "Who knows? Maybe it's a long-term relationship. Or maybe she's sick, and he feels like he can't leave her. I honestly have no idea. I don't really care, but he made his choice that day."

"I guess you know what that means."

Grayson forced a smile. "Find someone to make me forget him."

"You're learning."

"Finally," Grayson said as she reached over and turned up the radio. They drove to their favorite spot. She felt a little better getting it off her chest. Nothing some alcohol and random guy couldn't take care of. She was grateful Luna didn't give her a hard time about getting involved with Derrick.

They walked through the bar and there was a big group of guys surrounding the pool table.

Hot Damn.

Grayson nudged Luna, and she glanced over.

"Navy," she said matter-of-factly.

"Navy?" Grayson scrunched up her nose.

"No little sister, not just Navy. Navy SEAL's."

"What the hell are SEAL's doing here? There isn't any water around."

"I guess they just use the ranges here or something. Ethan can't stand them." Luna shrugged.

"Why?"

"Professional rivalry, and it goes both ways."

Interesting. If Ethan couldn't stand them, then there was a good chance Derrick felt the same way. A slow smile spread across her face.

They made their way to the bar, and the bartender pushed over their drinks without asking for their order.

Grayson tried to take in the guys. It should be illegal to have so many attractive men together at once.

One of the guys from the group made his way over to the table and stood next to them. He had tanned skin, light eyes, a shaved head and infectious smile.

He leaned down and spoke over the music. "I'm just going to stand here and buy your drinks. You don't have to talk to me."

"That's your line?" Luna laughed. "I have to admit it's pretty good."

"The big guy over there sent me over. I'm on wing man duty."

Grayson looked over. Most of them looked pretty big to her. "Which one?"

"The ugly redhead. I told him I couldn't tell the difference between you two, but he said he wants you," he said, pointing at Grayson.

"He wants me?" Grayson couldn't help but smile. Big ugly redhead? That sounded perfect to her right about now. It was hard to tell hair color from the distance and the dim light. "Tell him to come over here."

The guy took a swig of his beer, sat it down on the table, and then made his way back to the group. Grayson watched him talk to a burly man in the middle. He was big, but she couldn't tell if he was attractive or even if his hair really was red. A few guys slapped him on the back as he made his way over to their table.

"I'm not having sex with the bald one. There's no way I'm fucking the wingman," Luna said firmly.

"I don't care what you do. I want the ugly red," Grayson said as she watched them come forward. He was huge, over six foot and at least 220 lbs.

"There are a lot of them. I'm sure I can find one to entertain me for the evening," Luna yelled over the music and raised her bottle to her lips.

The big guy came over to her side of the table. She liked that he didn't pay attention to her sister. Usually guys made a stupid comment about never having twins or something equally as ridiculous. His hair was more auburn than red and made her think of Derrick. His face was wide, eyes light brown and his crooked nose had been broken more than once. His arms were covered in tattoos. Definitely not what she would call attractive. And yet she knew instantly she wanted to go home with him that evening.

"What's your name?" Grayson asked.

"Brick."

"Brick? I guess that's fitting. Obviously, not your real name?"

He smiled. "That's what everyone calls me. What's yours?"

"Should I make one up? Or tell you my real name?"

"I guess that's up to you."

"Grayson. That's my real name." He reached out his hand to shake hers. His hand was huge and callused. She was immediately turned on just by the touch of him.

Chemistry.

Luna went over and joined the group of guys leaving them alone. They spent the next couple of hours talking. The attraction between them was undeniable. After her fourth drink, Grayson leaned over and yelled over the noise, "I want you to take me to your room and fuck me like you own me."

"Don't say that unless you mean it," he practically growled back.

"Oh, I mean it."

He stood up leaned down and tossed her over his shoulder like a damn cave man and carried her out of the bar. Grayson was laughing and kicking telling him to put her down, or she was going to get sick. Once outside he set her down.

"Damn girl. You're about to give me a heart attack. Are you sure about this?"

"I'm sure. Let's go." She grabbed his hand, and they walked across the way to the hotel. The bar really was in an ideal location.

The door shut, and Brick pushed her against it. His hands were pressed on each side of her.

"You're fucking perfection," he told her, his body

firm against hers.

Her face was already flushed from the drinks, but she could feel the heat rise. What the hell was she doing? She found herself asking that question over and over these days.

He pulled her shirt over her head and unclasped her bra dropping it to the floor. One hand grabbed her breast, and his thumb roughly rubbed her taunt nipple in a circular motion. With the other hand, he pushed down her pants.

Grayson undid his pants and nearly gasped. He was huge and more than ready to go. She dropped down onto her knees and tried to take him all in, but that wasn't going to happen.

As if she weighed nothing he pulled her up and slid her onto him. She wrapped her legs around his waist and cried out. His large hands gripped her ass. Holy shit. He pushed her up against the door. "I'm going to fuck you all over this room."

Grayson moaned.

He tossed her onto the bed and turned her around. His hands nearly covered her whole waist. Before long, they were both slick with sweat. He carried her over to the chair got on his knees and tossed her legs over his shoulders. He spread her swollen lips apart, running his tongue up the sides of her, his roughened beard nearly driving her mad.

It was the most intense sex she had ever experienced, and after Derrick that was saying a lot. Where Derrick had always held back, Brick devoured her. Where Derrick made her feel powerless, Brick made her feel powerful.

He made her feel beautiful.

"What the hell are you doing with someone like

me?" he asked when they lay beside each other, catching their breath.

"What do you mean by that?"

"Look at me. You're way out of my league. You're gorgeous, and we'll, I'm me. It's like beauty and the beast."

"Why did you pick me and not my sister? Guys always want my sister."

He thought about it for a moment. "It was the way you walk."

Grayson tilted her head to look at him. "The way I walk?"

"Yeah, your sister walks like she knows everyone is looking at her, and she eats up the attention. You, on the other hand, are totally unaware of the effect you have on others. It's very sexy. You seem at ease with yourself and your surroundings."

Grayson nearly laughed. She never felt at ease with her surroundings, but she was glad she came across that way. Perception was reality.

Grayson turned over and ran her hand over his chest, stopping to feel an indent.

Brick grabbed her hand.

"What happened?" Grayson asked softly.

"Shot in Afghanistan. One of my buddies got killed. I went ballistic. I don't know how I'm alive."

Grayson leaned down and traced the scar with her lips and then climbed on top of him. She was surprised to feel the full length of him grow so quickly. She loved that she had that effect on him.

They literally did not sleep a wink that night.

The next morning, the door opened, and a cleaning lady walked in. Grayson's legs were thrown over his shoulders, her ankles grasped in his hands. He didn't stop; hell, he didn't even turn around. The woman covered her mouth, turned and left the room, giggling.

They both burst out laughing as soon as the door shut behind her.

"I guess we'll have to put the do not disturb sign on the door next time," Brick said.

"Next time? How long are you here for?"

"Two weeks. We just got here yesterday."

Grayson grinned. The idea of spending two weeks in his bed was very, very appealing. For the first time, she looked forward to seeing someone again. Well other than Derrick, but that obviously didn't end well. Two weeks she could handle. Maybe it would be possible to forget about Derrick. At least for a little while anyway.

Brick's phone buzzed, and he grabbed it off the table. "Shit," he said with a laugh. "I'm late for work. The guys are waiting for me outside."

"Sorry," Grayson said, smiling sheepishly.

He pulled her to him and kissed her deeply, causing every part of her body to tingle with desire. "Meet me tonight at the same place?"

Grayson nodded, reluctantly got out of bed, and pulled on her jeans.

"Thank you."

He laughed. "You're thanking me?"

"Yeah, I was in need of a distraction."

"A distraction huh? I'll take what I can get at this point," he said as he pulled her in and kissed her quickly.

Grayson was grinning from ear to ear when she made her way down to her Jeep. Her face fell when she saw she missed messages from Derrick. Why did she feel like she was cheating on him? That was beyond absurd. He was the one that left without saying good-

bye. He obviously chose the blonde over her. She would be stupid not to move on.

CHAPTER 30

She didn't know why, but she had kept Brick a secret from Derrick. It started to drive her crazy after a week, so she finally told him. Maybe it was out of spite. She wasn't even sure anymore. As pissed off as she was at Derrick, she still kept her phone in reaching distance just in case he messaged her. They chatted online for hours each day, which only confused her more. She felt like she was finally getting to know him, but he'd still left her without a proper good-bye. He chose someone else over her. It was as simple as that. And if nothing else, Brick was an escape from that harsh reality. She enjoyed hanging out with him and his friends. They were fun and lived in the moment. Being carefree and going with the flow was not something Grayson had ever been good at.

I haven't told you something. She hesitated for a moment and then hit send.

Oh?

I've been seeing someone for the last week.

Who?

A guy from out of town. She bit her lip as she pushed

send. For some reason, she wanted to make him mad like he had made her that day at the bookstore. *He's Navy.*

A fucking SEAL?

I guess. I never asked, but that's what Luna said.

Did you use protection?

Grayson covered her mouth and looked at the screen. She hesitated. The truth was she had not. It happened so quickly with Brick it never even crossed her mind. And after once what was the sense in worrying about it? They had talked about it later, and Brick insisted he was clean that they get checked every six months. She believed him but would be sure to go to her doctor before she was with anyone else. Plus, as far as she had been concerned her time with Derrick was over. He forfeited his right the day he looked away. Before she had time to form a reply Derrick's message chimed.

I see.

What does that mean?

I have to go.

Of course you do. You always run away don't you? Are you angry?

Nope.

God forbid you show some emotion. Need I remind you that you had your chance and blew it?

Why did you lie about it?

I didn't lie. I just didn't tell you. I guess I felt guilty, like I was cheating on you, which is absurd.

Me too.

Me too what? You feel like I cheated on you?

I know it's not fair, but yes. I had secretly hoped you would wait for me.

That's not fair! How can you say that? Do you not

recall how we left things? You didn't even say good-bye to me.

Free will, Gray.

Screw you and your goddamn free will. Derrick you are driving me fucking crazy. All I do is think about you, everyday, all day long.

Obviously not if you've been fucking a SEAL for a week.

Grayson inhaled sharply. She didn't know how to respond. *If you want me to not see him again I won't, but only if you agree not to see the blonde.*

You can have sex with whomever you want Grayson.

I guess I can. And by the way, he's got a 10" cock and fucks me like I belong to him. Grayson hit send and waited, but no reply came. A few moments later Derrick signed offline.

How did this get so complicated? It was supposed to be an easy, no-strings-attached relationship. She should have known better. She wasn't made for those sorts of relationships. She buried her head in her hands and fought the tears from falling. But it was useless.

How could I be such a fool, Grayson thought, *I never should have done any of this to begin with. Now I'm left with nothing but heartache.* No matter how amazing the sex was with Brick, it was Derrick who she longed for.

Later that evening, Grayson and Luna made their way to the bowling alley to meet Brick and his friends. After her argument with Derrick, Grayson really didn't want to go out, but they had already made plans. And Luna loved to bowl, so she had to go.

She sent a text to Brick letting him know they were on their way. When they pulled up, he was waiting for her outside. A smile spread across his face when he saw her, and she was glad she decided to show up. She loved the attention Brick heaped on her.

He walked across the parking lot to meet them. "You look incredible," he said. He threw his arm around her shoulder, and she draped her arm around his waist. Brick told her he loved being seen in public with her. That he felt like a rooster with his chest all puffed out when she was by his side. Brick's PDA was the complete opposite of Derrick and Grayson's interactions. She had to admit it was flattering.

Luna rolled her eyes, and they made their way to the group of guys who had already started bowling.

"Watch Mason. He takes bowling very seriously." Brick laughed. "He brings his own shoes with him on the road. It's ridiculous."

"Is that so?" Luna clapped her hands together. "I guess I'm going to have to kick his ass."

Brick gave Grayson a look that caused her to giggle. Luna really was a good bowler so it would be interesting to watch.

"Your shoes are at the table."

"How'd you know our shoe size?" Grayson asked surprised.

"You left your flip flops one morning. They were so tiny I had to check the size."

Once they reached the table their drinks were handed to them, and Luna started trash talking trying to get Mason all riled up. Knowing Luna, they would probably end up in bed before the night was over.

Brick pulled Grayson onto his lap. His large hand slid up her shirt and Grayson leaned in kissing him slowly at first and then deeper. He was just the distraction she needed.

The hell with Derrick.

"Get a room!" one of the guys yelled and then a few of them clicked glasses.

"I don't think I can wait that long," Grayson whispered into his ear. "Let's go into the bathroom."

"You're killing me, girl."

Grayson hoped off his lap, took a shot of whiskey and walked towards the men's room.

"Brick it's your turn," someone yelled.

"I'll be missing this game," Brick said pulling her close, not bothering to turn around.

"Jesus! How'd that bastard get so lucky?" Grayson heard one of the guys mutter.

Sex in a public bathroom. This is definitely a first. Grayson smiled to herself.

Brick pushed her up against the cold tile wall his mouth trailed down her neck. Reaching down she stroked his hard cock through his pants.

"Grayson," he groaned, his mouth against her skin. The feel of his mouth made her shiver.

He lifted her as if she weighed nothing. His hand roamed under her shirt. Her breathing was ragged, and she wanted him badly. Grayson pressed her legs tighter around his waist. Her arms encircled his neck and she ran a hand through his hair. Meanwhile, Brick was still busy under her shirt. His other hand dug into her thigh, and she moaned.

Grayson sucked on the bottom on his lip, and Brick kissed her back his breath growing raged.

The door creaked open, and a big bald man walked in clearing his throat.

"Hey, man. I hate to do this, but she can't be in

here."

Grayson's face turned bright red, and she buried her head in Brick's neck. He slowly lowered her to the ground.

"We're not done," Brick said hoarsely.

"If it was up to me, I'd let you stay all night, but this is a public restroom."

Grayson pulled her shirt down and was glad no clothes had been removed yet. "It's fine we'll finish in the car."

"Lucky bastard," the bouncer said, shaking his head with a grin

"Don't I know it," Brick said as he smirked and grabbed her hand. They made their way outside and hurried to the parking lot to finish what they had started.

When they got back inside they were finished bowling and already in the bar. Arms wrapped around each other, Brick pushed her up against the bar and crushed his lips to hers.

"I've never been one for PDA, but I want everyone here to know you're with me," Brick said roughly and kissed her again.

They listened to Karaoke and drank a lot.

Suddenly Brick jumped up, and Grayson had no idea what was going on. Next thing she knew Brick had some guy on the ground, and his fist smashed twice into the guys face. Blood poured down the guy's mouth it looked as if the side of his face had been crushed.

Grayson moved closer. Brick's hand was raised to hit the guy again.

"Brick!" Their eyes met, and Grayson shook her head no. Brick dropped the guy to the ground and came to her.

"What the hell just happened?"

"I'm sorry you had to see that. I don't want you to see me like that."

"Why did you hit him?"

"He pushed Mason," Brick said and looked away.

"Pushed him? I didn't see anything are you sure he didn't just bang into him? This place is packed."

Some of the guys were crowded around them now and pulling them to the other side of the bar.

"We need to stay over here in case the cops come. You busted that guys jaw. He'll probably have to have it wired back together," Danny said over the music.

Grayson was confused, and more than a little freaked out. Unless she had missed something completely there was no need for the show of violence, and she was pretty sure Mason could take care of himself anyway.

Mason looked embarrassed. Grayson pulled away from Brick and walked over to Mason.

"Did that guy start a fight with you?"

"No. Brick overreacted as usual. The guy thought I was hitting on his girl and came over to confront me. It was nothing. I had it taken care of. "

Grayson looked back over at Brick, and he was laughing with his friends.

What the hell? That seemed like something a high school kid would do. Not a grown ass man.

"He does that a lot?" Grayson asked, frowning. She really didn't know anything about Brick after all.

"He loves bar brawls. It seems like he gets in at least one every time we go out of town."

Great.

"At least he stopped when you told him too. It could

have been a lot worse. "

"Worse? The guy's jaw looked shattered," Grayson said, suddenly feeling ill and wanting to go home.

Brick waved her over. Grayson looked around for Luna, but didn't see her anywhere.

Grayson made her way back to Brick.

He leaned down and said, "Sorry."

As if she was the one he should be saying he was sorry to. About fifteen minutes later a couple of cops walked in and scanned the bar talking to a few people. No one pointed towards them. Grayson wasn't sure if they were afraid to or just didn't want to help the cops, but either way Brick was lucky. Eventually, the cops walked out and some of the guys fist bumped Brick. Grayson rolled her eyes.

She had drunk too much to drive home, so she ended up going back to the hotel with Brick. Even though she suddenly found him less attractive after the display at the bowling alley.

CHAPTER 31

A week passed, and she hadn't heard anything from Derrick. She'd sent him a couple of emails and messages, but he didn't reply. They really were over. It made her feel sick. Deep down, she'd really thought they had something more than just sex.

Brick went back to Virginia the night before, and she was glad he was gone. He was exhausting. She barely got any sleep for two weeks, and he turned out to be obnoxious. The sex was incredible, but that was all there was to it. She could never see herself in a real relationship with him. He wanted to keep in touch, but she told him it was two weeks of fun. The fool tried to tell her he was in love with her. Grayson had laughed and said he loved fucking her, and he didn't know the first thing about her. Which was the truth. They were truly about sex.

Although, hadn't she thought the same about Derrick? Love really was an overused word. Hell, she didn't even know if she comprehended the full meaning of love. At one point she'd thought she was in love with Josh. Maybe what she felt for Derrick wasn't real either.

As she wiped down the kitchen counter Grayson got a bad feeling in the pit of her stomach so bad that it almost dropped her to her knees. She felt like she was going to crawl out of her skin, and Derrick's name screamed through her head. A wave of nausea washed over her. Something was wrong, and Grayson was scared shitless.

Ever since she had been a kid, Grayson instincts warned her when something bad happened to people she was close to. Once a friend of the family had been in a car accident, and she ran in the house crying that Uncle Mike was hurt. Her mom tried to console her. She finally got hold of his wife, and Cindy informed them Mike was in the hospital and might not ever walk again. Another time her father was out on the ship, and Grayson knew he'd hurt his arm. She told her mom and when her mother talked to her father, she found out he had badly burned his arm, and the worst was when she knew her grandmother was dying. That was what this feeling she was having felt like.

Tears streamed down her face and agony flowed through her. She picked up the phone and called Heather.

"Did anyone get hurt on the team?"

"Grayson, why are you asking that?" Heather's voice raised several notches.

"Just a weird feeling, that's all. If you hear anything let me know."

"You're scaring me, Grayson. Ethan has told me about your freaky sixth sense thing. Do you think something happened to Ethan?"

"No, no. Not Ethan." What the hell had she been thinking calling Heather? Of course, she was going to assume it was Ethan. "Derrick. I think something happened to him."

"Derrick?" Heather asked, confused but considerably calmer.

"Yeah, we've spent some time together. But we kept it a secret."

"Oh, Grayson. Okay, let me make some calls and see if I can find out anything. However, I've heard nothing so far so I think you're mistaken this time."

"I hope so. I really hope so," Grayson said and clicked off the phone.

But, she knew she wasn't wrong. The cold pit at the bottom of her stomach would not go away. *Could Derrick really be dead?*

She turned on the news and couldn't find anything. Online she searched deaths in Afghanistan, but nothing from today. She sent a few messages to Ethan's Skype and paced the house. She was glad her mother wasn't home to see her such a wreck.

Several hours later Heather called her back. "Grayson, you're freaking me out here. You know I can't talk about that stuff even if something did happen."

Her stomach twisted. If nothing had happened, she would have told her everything was fine, and she was overreacting. The worst part was they had kept their relationship a secret. No one even knew how crazy she was about him.

"Just tell me is Derrick alive?" She asked, her voice cracking.

"Grayson, I know you have your little witchy thing going on, but I can't tell you anything. All I can say to you is that there has been an incident. Turn on the news and you'll see."

She dropped to her knees and she just knew he was gone. He was gone and she never got to tell him how she felt about him. They hadn't even given their relationship a real chance. All because of her stupid fucking rules.

Forcing herself to her feet Grayson made her way to the living room. Everything seemed to be moving in slow motion. Grabbing the remote she turned back on the television and flipped to fox news. She covered her mouth as she heard the newscaster speak. "Breaking news: Two Special Forces soldiers were killed in Afghanistan during a raid. Names will not be released until family members are notified."

No. No. No. No! She mumbled shaking her head. This couldn't be real. Grayson ran into her room, and threw herself on the bed crying. Her body shook with heart-wrenching sobs from her head to her toes.

Finally, when she thought she could talk, she called her sister Luna and filled her in on everything. Her sister rushed over and threw her arms around her.

She couldn't believe this was happening, and the last conversation they had they were fighting. All because of some stupid sexual relationship she had that meant nothing to her.

Somehow she made it through the day, and her phone woke her around three thirty in the morning. She recognized the out of country code. She braced herself to hear the news.

"Ethan?"

"Grayson, you didn't hear this from me."

"Okay."

"Derrick died."

Grayson closed her eyes, and hot tears silently fell.

"But they brought him back to life. He's been medevac'd out of here, but it doesn't look good. His injuries are extensive. They don't think he's going to make it."

He's alive? That was all she heard all that mattered to her. He had a chance.

"Was something going on with you two? I know you get these feelings, but it's usually only about someone important to you."

There was no sense in lying about it anymore. "We had been seeing each other on and off for months."

"I thought that might be the case. He'd been acting different lately."

"How so?"

"No more bragging about his sexual conquests. I thought he was going through a dry spell."

"What about the blonde?"

"The blonde?" Ethan sounded confused. "You mean Megan?"

"I don't know her name."

"She's just some girl on their endurance team. I think they used to have a thing, but nothing serious. She was kind of psycho if I recall. He was definitely not into her the way she was into him."

Grayson let the information sink in. If they didn't currently have a thing going on, why had he led her to believe they did? None of it made sense. And now, she might never know.

"Is there any way I can talk to him?"

"Not now. Grayson, don't get your hopes up. It's a miracle they could revive him. If he lives he owes his life to Marcus, the medic."

"I just need to tell him something."

"They sent him to Germany and are operating now.

If he wakes up and can take calls I'll let you know."

"Thank you."

"You can't tell *anyone*. All the family members of the one who got killed haven't been notified yet."

"I understand," Grayson said and clicked off the phone. So many emotions were running through her. She was elated that Derrick was alive, confused about the girl, and terrified he wasn't going to make it.

She hadn't even asked what his injuries were. Worst-case scenarios raced through her mind, but none of that mattered. If he would have her, she would stick by him no matter what.

CHAPTER 32

Three long days later, her brother called her with a phone number.

Grayson's hand shook as she dialed the number. A woman with a southern accent answered the phone. Maybe it's a nurse she thought, or his mother. However, a bigger part of her feared it was Megan, and her brother was wrong.

"Can I speak to Derrick?"

"He's asleep. If you give me your number I'll tell him when he wakes up."

Grayson rattled off her number, and wondered if he would call.

Two days passed, and he didn't return her call. She was miserable. Grabbing the phone she took a chance to call again. This time he answered. He sounded groggy. "Hello."

"It's Gray."

"Oh. Hey."

She couldn't help it. She started crying. "I'm so sorry Derrick."

"Don't be."

"Derrick. I know this isn't the right time to say this, but I need you to know. I'm in love with you and I have been probably since our eyes met in the coffee shop."

She was met with silence, and then he said, "It's funny how tragedies make people say things they wouldn't normally say."

"I mean it, Derrick," Grayson told him while she rubbed her nose with the back of her shirt. "I wanted to say it before you left, but I never got the chance."

"I need to go. I'm tired."

"Derrick? Please."

"I'll call you later." And he clicked off the phone.

Grayson sat staring at her phone in disbelief. She poured her heart out to him and he basically hung up on her. Although, what did she expect? She still had no idea how extensive his injuries were. One of his friends had just been killed. She shouldn't have said anything about her feelings. It wasn't the right time.

Idiot.

A week passed before he called. She had no idea how she made it through the week. It passed painfully slow she just went through the motions.

"I'm in Washington, DC, at Bethesda hospital."

Grayson's pulse raced. "Thank god. I'm going to leave tonight and come see you."

"Don't bother."

A lump formed in her throat. "Derrick, you don't mean that."

"Yes, I do. I don't want to see you or anyone else. I just want to be alone."

Closing her eyes, she took a deep breath. She had

to do this on his timeline. Grayson spoke when she finally found her voice again, "Okay. I'll respect that, but if you change your mind, I'll jump in the Jeep or on a plane. I really want to see you."

"I don't want anyone seeing me like this."

Grayson braced herself. She had asked Ethan, but he had been vague. "What are your injuries?"

"I'm alive and have all my limbs. That's all that matters. Andrews wasn't so lucky."

"I'm sorry," she said, struggling to find the right words, but she had nothing. In this situation, there were no words that could make his pain hurt less. He lost a friend and almost his own life. She wondered if he was suffering from survivor's guilt.

"I wasn't going to call you."

"I'm glad you did."

"You're so deep under my skin it's driving me crazy," he said through clenched teeth, like it pissed him off.

"I know the feeling," she replied, her heart speeding up like crazy. Maybe there was hope for them after all.

"I don't think you do."

"When can you come home?"

"No idea. I have a long recovery ahead of me. Probably months."

That took her by surprise. His injuries must be really bad if they wouldn't transfer him to the local military hospital. She wanted to press him, but she'd ask Ethan later.

"I hope you'll let me come see you eventually," she said.

"We'll see. I need to sleep, but I wanted to return the call."

"Derrick, I meant what I said."

"Don't. I can't handle that right now."

Grayson sucked in a breath and released it slowly, "Alright."

They talked a couple more minutes and then hung up.

The first thing Grayson did was call Luna to fill her in.

"Screw that get in your Jeep and go—now," Luna said.

"He doesn't want me there. He made that painfully clear." Her emotions were pulling her in different directions. She wanted to be by his side, but also felt she should listen to what he wanted.

"Grayson if you feel the way I think you do about this guy, just go. He just thinks he doesn't want you there. Trusts me. He'll be glad you came."

Maybe she was right. Hell, their whole relationship made no sense. Why should this be any different?

"You're right. I'm going to go."

"Good luck!"

Grayson looked around and threw a few days clothes in a bag. She had a flash of déjà vu of when she was leaving Josh. Instead of running away this time she was running to someone. She had to see him, even if he kicked her out.

She left her mother a note, jumped into the Jeep, and punched in the address of the VA hospital in DC. It was going to be a long drive.

The next evening she pulled into the hospital parking lot. Her stomach was in knots. What was he going to do when he saw her? He was probably going to be

pissed for one.

She made her way to the reception desk and asked for Derrick O'Conner. The nurse tapped his name into the computer and told her the room number. "Visiting hours end in an hour."

Grayson nodded and crossed the hall towards the elevator. She could feel the tension increase with every step.

She stood in front of room 1303. The door was shut. Taking a deep breath she tapped on the door and pushed through it. And then her world came crashing down—again. Her steps faltered. She really was a fool.

Sitting in the chair next to Derrick was the blonde.

Derrick's eyes fluttered opened. A look of surprised flashed. "What are you doing here? I told you not to come," he said, sounding exhausted. Half his face was covered with a large bandage.

Swallowing hard she tried to push back the tears. She didn't know what to say.

"Megan, can you go get me something to eat?"

The girl narrowed her eyes at Grayson and then stood up and stalked out of the room.

"Obviously, I made a mistake," Grayson said her voice shook, betraying her emotions.

Derrick tried to pull himself up to sit, but it took too much effort, so he gave up.

Grayson took in all the machines attached to him. He looked like he had lost a lot of weight. His skin was so pale, and his eyes were dark and sad. She knew she was being selfish, but she was hurt. It felt like he had twisted a knife through her heart.

"I guess when you said you didn't want company, you meant everyone but your girlfriend."

"She's not..."

Grayson held up her hand to cut him off and said, "Enough with all the lies Derrick. I'm an idiot." A tear fell and she wiped it away with the back of her hand. "I'm sorry you're hurt, but you were right, I shouldn't have come here. Next time I'll listen." She turned to leave.

"Gray, don't go. She just showed up. I don't even know how she knew I was here. One of the wives on the team must have told her."

Heart pounding, she slowly turned back towards him. He licked his cracked lips and reached for the water, but it was out of his reach. Grayson hurried forward, grabbed the drink and held it out so he could drink from the straw.

"That's why I didn't want you here," he said as he leaned back and closed his eyes.

"Because of her? You didn't want me to come because your little girlfriend is already here taking care of you?"

"No Gray, not because of her. I can't even get my own water. I don't want you seeing me like this. It's humiliating."

"That's ridiculous. You're hurt. You almost died. There is nothing humiliating about that."

"I'm a mess. I can't even go to the bathroom by myself."

She knew that guys like Derrick didn't like the loss of control.

Grayson leaned forward and ran her hand through his hair. His face was covered in red stubble, and he looked completely drained.

"Tomorrow is the funeral at Arlington," he said so softly Grayson had to strain to hear the words.

"And you can't go." She grabbed his hand from

under the blanket. His hand was so cold in hers. She had to do something to help him. She whispered in his ear. "Do you want me to go for you?"

"You didn't even know him," he choked out.

"No, but I know my brother. I know you. I know the sacrifice the families of soldiers make."

His eyes welled with tears. He looked away, clearing his throat.

What the hell was she doing coming in here like this? The last thing Derrick needed to worry about was some crazy-ass girl. She needed to push her jealousy aside and just be there for him. Even if they only ended up being friends, and nothing more, she had to forget all that right now.

Leaning down she kissed the top of his forehead. "I should have respected your wishes."

"I'm glad you didn't."

With a faint whisper of hope in her voice she asked, "Really?"

He nodded. "Thanks for coming to see me."

The door burst open, and Megan came through the door holding a tray.

Grayson shifted beneath her feet uncomfortable and not sure what to do. *Talk about awkward.* She still had his hand in hers, and she didn't want to let go.

"Thanks, Megan. Why don't you go back to your room? I want to visit with Grayson for a few more minutes and then get some sleep."

Megan eyed Grayson as she set the tray down. "I got your favorites."

"Thank you."

Megan stood there for a moment and then turned to grab her jacket off the back of a chair. "I'll be back in the morning then," she said in a rather bitchy tone.

"You really should go home, Megan. There is nothing you can do here."

"I want to be here."

"My parents are going to arrive tomorrow. And I'd prefer not to have anyone else here."

Megan looked down at the floor. "Okay. Well, I'll come have breakfast with you before I leave."

"That's fine."

She hesitated like she wanted to say something, but turned and walked out the door.

Derrick closed his eyes and sighed. "I wish she'd never shown up."

"I'm so confused Derrick. I don't know what to believe anymore. You have me questioning what I see right in front of my face."

"I'm sorry. It's really not what it looks like."

"You keep saying that but offer no explanation. I was warned you were a ladies' man, but why is it always the same girl? It makes no sense."

"She's a friend. And unfortunately, she feels more for me than I do her. That's all I'm going to say about this right now."

Grayson wanted to press the issue, but kept her mouth shut. They could sort this mess out later for now she was just happy that he wanted her there, and not Megan.

"I'm tired, Gray. My brain hurts. I keep going over what happened in my mind. Could I have done something different? Why did Andrews die and not me? I know everyone's life has an expiration date. It's just hard to come to terms with it all."

Grayson looked over at Derrick and felt her heart lurch. The pain in his expression was difficult to see.

How could she be so selfish when he was obviously in turmoil?

CHAPTER 33

Dressed in a dark charcoal dress Grayson made her way down the aisle searching for a seat. There were so many people and even camera crews. Military funerals were enough to pull at anyone's heart strings. Ethan saw her and waved her over. He looked so handsome in his dress blues. Why hadn't she thought about Ethan being there? Probably because she had been incapable to think clearly since Derrick had been injured. Hell, she hadn't been able to think straight since the day she laid eyes on Derrick.

She was grateful to see a familiar face. Grayson made her way over and sat in between her brother and Marcus. Seeing her brother made her feel better. She was a ball of nerves all morning.

"I didn't even know you were back," she whispered.

"Only Marcus and I could come to the funeral the others had to stay back. Luna told me you were in DC, but I didn't expect to see you here."

"I just felt like I should be here."

Marcus leaned over and whispered, "Look who's coming."

They all turned, and Grayson's mouth dropped open. Derrick was being wheeled down the lawn. An IV bag was hung above him, and he looked very weak. He was in his uniform, and had shaved. Grayson wanted to jump up and run to him, but Ethan grabbed her hand and squeezed it. "He needs to do this alone," he said in a low voice. Grayson nodded she knew he was right. It was not her place to be by his side.

Her eyes were glued to him as he was pushed to the front. A beautiful woman stood up and walked over to him. She was tall, slim with long dark hair, and was holding a baby.

"Andrews's wife," Marcus whispered.

Grayson felt like she was prying seeing the exchange. The woman leaned down to hug Derrick, and stood up and wiped her eyes. Grayson was moved by the woman's strength. It couldn't be easy seeing Derrick knowing he was alive, and her husband was gone. The same thing was probably running through Derrick's mind. Her heart ached for him.

She took the wheel chair from the nurse and pushed him to the front beside her. It was a touching moment, and Grayson realized her cheeks were wet.

The next-day Grace was antsy sitting around the empty hotel room. She decided to go back to the hospital before she drove home. As much as she wanted to be there she knew she was not welcome, and it was rude of her to have intruded on Derrick out of her own selfish need to see him. She didn't approach him at the funeral or even later that day. She knew he needed to be with his family and friends. Sadly, she didn't seem to fit into either category.

She pushed through the door and was relieved to see that he was alone. She didn't think she could handle another run-in with Megan, and it would be strange to meet his parents. She stared at him for a minute her throat tightening with affection.

"Hey," Derrick said. He looked up and clicked the remote and turned off the TV.

She walked over and stood next to his bed. "How are you doing?"

He shrugged. "Not so great. Yesterday was rough."

She sat down in a chair next to him and pulled it closer to the bed. "I could tell his wife appreciated you showing up."

"You were there? I didn't see you."

"I didn't think it was right to approach you."

He just nodded.

Grayson sat in silence not sure what to say. The only noise was the steady hum of the fluorescent lights, and an occasional beep of the machines attached to him.

"Thanks for coming. I know I told you not to, but I'm glad you did."

"Really? I thought you were still mad at me."

"I am, but not for coming here. I would have done the same thing if the situation had been reversed."

That brought a smile to her face. "How long are you going to be here?"

"A couple of months at least; I have a lot of rehab to get through."

"Do you want me to stay? I haven't started school yet."

He shook his head no. "I need to be alone. I have a lot of stuff going on in my head; I need to get it all sorted out. When I get back we'll sit down and talk."

She could feel tears starting to form so she tried to blink them back. She didn't want him to see her cry. "I understand. I'm going to drive back today."

"Gray. How did you know I was hurt? I've heard some stuff, but I'm not sure if the guys were pulling my leg or not."

She shifted on the seat uncomfortably as she watched a play of emotions cross his face. "I just knew."

"What do you mean you just knew?"

"I don't know it's weird. My mother says everyone has the ability, but they don't listen to the vibrations from the earth. Kind of like when someone walks into a bad situation and the hair on the back of their neck stands up. Or for some reason, a person decides to take the back way home instead of their normal path and misses being in an accident. I just sometimes know things like that. I never tell anyone because it makes me sound like a freak."

He gave her a half smile that melted her heart and said, "It is kind of freaky. You've never told anyone?"

"Well, my family obviously knows. It's been happening since I was a child."

"What about your ex?"

Grayson shook her head no. "He thinks anything that is not explainable is stupid."

"He's an idiot. So tell me exactly what happened."

"Well, I was just going about my day as normal and suddenly your name screamed through my head, and I felt like crying. My stomach dropped causing my heart to race rapidly. I started calling around trying to find out what happened, but at first no one would tell me anything. It's happened to me before, but only with people I'm close to. I thought you were dead."

"I guess I was, briefly anyway."

She tilted her head and asked what she was sure everyone else had already asked, "Did you see a white light?"

"Not that I recall. I do know I woke up thinking about you. I reached for the pendant, and it was gone."

"You got the pendant? I didn't know if you saw it or would know it was from me."

"I knew." He smiled sadly. "Who else would think to get me the perfect present? Marcus says the pendant saved my life."

"And here I was thinking it was Marcus, I had to thank," Grayson grinned.

"Maybe it was a bit of both." Derrick closed his eyes, "I was so pissed at you."

"I still don't understand why you were mad." Grayson pulled at the edge of her sweater.

"I can't talk about this now. I'm starting to get pissed just thinking about it."

"I'm sorry." She looked up at the monitor, and his heart rate was elevated.

"If you had just shown up before you left..."

"Seriously, not now Grayson I beg you. I don't want to say something I'll regret."

"You're right." Grayson stood up and leaned over the bed. Lightly, she touched her lips to his. His lips were cracked and dry, but they felt so good. He parted his mouth, and Grayson ran her hand down the side of his face. He was going to have a lot of scars, but to her, he had never looked more beautiful. She pulled away, "I guess I should go."

"Do you have to leave right now?" He asked surprising her.

"Nope. I'm driving so it doesn't matter when I

leave," Grayson answered him and smiled hesitantly. Did he want her to stay?

"As much as I would love to ravish your body, that's not going to happen." Derrick gave her a crooked grin. "But, I wouldn't mind the company."

Grayson lowered herself back into the seat. Hopefully, this was a positive sign. Maybe they had a chance of working this out after all.

"What are you watching?"

"CSI. I've never seen it before I got in here and they're having a marathon."

"I haven't seen it either. I don't really watch much TV."

"Me neither. I'd rather read over watching TV any day."

Grayson looked around and didn't see any books. She would stop in the gift shop and grab some for him before she left.

"Can you get that bag in the corner?"

Grayson looked over and there was a black duffle bag on the floor. She stood up and collected it and set it on the side of his bed.

"The guys grabbed the stuff out of my room and sent it over. I got you something."

"You got me something in Afghanistan?" She asked eyes wide.

He winced as he rummaged through the bag. He pulled out a huge chunk of lapis lazuli.

"Oh my god Derrick! It's gorgeous!"

He held it out for her, and she grabbed it.

"How did you know?" She ran her hand over the rough blue and gold rock.

"You said you started your degree for Geology, so I figured you'd like it. And I saw all the crystals in your room. When we arrived, one of the guys from the other team had a bunch of them. I guess they found them in caves. I grabbed one for you."

"Get out of here! They found them inside caves?" Grayson couldn't stop running her hands over the rough stone. "Did you know lapis is the stone of truth?"

"I did not."

"Well it is. It's supposed to bring harmony to relationships. In the middle east, it's believed to have magical powers."

"Interesting."

"You have no idea how much this means to me. Thank you." Grayson leaned down and kissed him again. "It's my new favorite."

Derrick sort of grunted and looked away his jaw clenched.

"What was that for?" She wondered what she had said that bothered him.

"Favorite? Are you sure about that? From the sounds of it, Navy boy is your new favorite."

"That guy was an obnoxious idiot. I was just trying to piss you off."

"Well, it worked. So are you saying he didn't have a ten-inch cock or fucked you like you belonged to him? I believe those were your exact words."

Grayson felt her face flush, and she couldn't meet his eyes.

"That's what I thought."

"Derrick, he meant nothing. I never even kept in touch with him."

He leaned back and closed his eyes. "I can't talk about this right now."

"I didn't mean to upset you, but we're going to have to talk about all of this at some point."

"And I told you we would. Just not right now."

"Alright. Well, I really do love the lapis lazuli."

"I'm glad you like it."

"I love it."

Derrick scooted to the side. "Get up here."

"Are you sure? I don't want to pull out your IV or anything."

He held his arm up, and Grayson climbed into the bed with him. They were pretty squished, but she wouldn't be anywhere else. She laid her head on his chest, and they watched television for hours.

By his heavy breathing, Grayson realized Derrick had dozed off. Quietly, she slid off the bed.

She nudged him, and his eyes fluttered open. "I'm going to go. Thank you for allowing me to visit."

Derrick squeezed her hand. "I'll keep in touch. "

"I hope so." Grayson leaned down and kissed him. She hurried down the hall to the gift shop and grabbed a handful of new release novels, and a few snacks.

By the time she got back to his room he was back to sleep. She wrote him a quick note. *Hurry home, Gray.*

CHAPTER 34

Two months later, the doorbell rang. Grayson was in the middle of writing a paper for school. She was as irritated at the interruption as she was relieved. Even if it was someone selling something, it was a distraction to get her eyes off the screen for a few minutes. School was fun, but it was a lot of work.

Grayson set her computer down and stretched before crossing the living room to open the door.

Nothing could have prepared her for Derrick standing on the other side.

She covered her mouth, breathless at the sight of him. He was still leaner than before the accident, but he looked great. His hair was slightly longer, and his face was covered in stubble, hiding most of the scars. His eyes were intense as ever, and maybe a little apprehensive. Not a look she was used to seeing on him.

She hesitated before taking a step back and holding open the door. He brushed passed her and went into the living room.

"Is your mother home?" He looked around, his

watchful gaze taking in the small house.

"She's gone for the weekend. Yoga retreat, again."

One of the cats wrapped itself around his legs, purring. He leaned down to pet it, avoiding her eyes as he said softly, "We need to talk."

Grayson's heart pounded. She took a deep breath before she replied, "I agree."

They were silent as Grayson settled onto the couch, and Derrick took an armchair next to her. The space between them felt like a void.

Derrick spoke first. "I've been doing a lot of thinking over the past two months. Well, hell, the past four months."

"Me, too—"

Derrick cut her off. "Let me finish. If I don't get this out now, I might never. This isn't easy for me."

Crossing her legs on the couch, Grayson turned towards Derrick, giving him her complete attention. She wondered if he was about to dump her, then berated herself because it wasn't like they were exactly a couple. She wasn't sure she could handle that, but they needed to figure something out. They couldn't go on like they had been.

"I haven't been honest with you."

Her heart dropped. She knew it. All the evasiveness, not to mention seeing him with that blonde chick ... Grayson forced herself to meet his eyes.

"I live with Megan, but I wasn't lying when I said she wasn't my girlfriend."

Anger rose in her chest. "What the hell does that mean?"

"Let me back up and try to explain."

"Please do." Grayson spat back as she crossed her arms and leaned back on the couch cushion. A million thoughts were racing through her mind as she waited for him to continue. Had their whole relationship been one big lie? Did he ever have feelings for her? Was she just another notch on his belt?

"I met Megan a couple of years ago. She's on our racing team. Most races need a female, so we put an ad out on the Internet, and she replied. At first, it was just training, but then one thing led to another, and we started a sexual relationship. She was more into me then I was with her. But, I was upfront that we weren't exclusive, and she was fine with that. Or at least she claimed to be. It wasn't until recently she's been acting crazy." He paused. "After I met you."

"Years?" Grayson stared at him in disbelief. "You've been with her for two years, and you don't consider her your girlfriend? How long have you lived together?" She almost felt bad for the girl. Almost.

"A few months."

"And you're still having sex with her?"

"Rarely."

Grayson clenched her jaw briefly, tempted to throttle him. "Rarely. Oh, well, that makes everything okay."

"You're not one to toss stones. You haven't exactly been Miss Innocent in all of this. I recall you leaving with two men at bars, not to mention the SEAL."

"But I was honest with you. You *lied* to me. Looked me straight in the face and lied to me. Over and over again," Grayson's voice rose with each word she spoke.

"Calm down, Gray. I'm trying to be honest with you, and it's not easy. I've never been one to explain myself to others. I only moved in with her because I was getting deployed for three months, my lease was getting ready to run out, and I would only be back in the States for three months before I left again. She offered her place, and I accepted. It seemed like a good idea at the time. It saved me money, and I didn't have to keep putting stuff in storage. It was an arrangement. That was how I saw it. An arrangement and nothing more."

"Did you have your own room?"

Derrick looked away. "No."

"And you had the nerve to get pissed off at me?" Grayson clenched her fist at her side. "I can't do this anymore."

"Gray." He reached out to touch her, but she pulled away.

"Don't call me that. Why did I let myself fall for you? I knew it was stupid. Heather warned me. My sister warned me, but I didn't listen. I couldn't listen. You were like some damn addiction. I couldn't get enough of you. The more you pulled away, the more I wanted you."

Reaching for her hand, he said, "It's the same for me. The day you laid your stupid rules out, I knew you were bad news. But, there was something about you. I just couldn't walk away. Believe me. I tried, several times."

"Chemistry?" she said bitterly.

He shook his head. "Chemistry fades. It's got to be more than physical attraction." He traced the curve of her upper lip, and she trembled at his touch. Taking her hand, Derrick caressed her skin with his thumb. "I want you, Gray. I've always wanted you."

"Obviously not enough," she said pulling away from his grasp, tucking her hands beneath her thighs.

"That's not true. I was confused. I'm used to being on my own and not getting deeply involved. It's always been about sex for me. I used women. I'm a selfish bastard. The way you make me feel scares the hell out of me. You're a chink in the armor."

Grayson rolled her eyes. "What does that even mean?"

"Like, you were warned. I never settle down. I haven't wanted to after my ex cheated on me. I never wanted to feel that vulnerable again. Hell, I can't even recall most of the girls' names I've been with."

"What about Megan?"

"I know it doesn't make sense to you. It doesn't really make sense to me either. I thought of her as a friend. She's like one of the guys. She's got a lot of issues, but I've never felt anything for her. I don't even really like her, but she was nice enough to help me out, and I took advantage of it. She knew I dated other women. She didn't care. I guess I started acting different once I met you."

"Different how exactly?"

"For one, I stopped seeing other women and kept you a secret. Another thing, I think in the last five or six months since we met, Megan and I only had sex twice. And trust me, she's very persistent."

Grayson couldn't help the twist in her stomach at the thought of him with another woman. "I don't get why you told me you lived with a guy on your team, a guy who had a child."

Derrick shrugged. "I'm a liar, Gray. I used the same line on everyone, and it was just a habit. My training goes with the mentality: you tell a lie, and you take it to the grave. Sometimes I can't stand to look at myself in the mirror. So I don't expect you to still want to be with me. I just felt I owed you the truth."

Grayson let the information sink in. As angry and

hurt as she felt, the reality was she hadn't behaved much better herself. They were a mess.

"Are you sure you don't have more feelings for Megan then you want to admit?" she asked softly.

Derrick laughed bitterly. "I'm positive."

"Well, you must like her to be in her company so often."

"Not necessarily. I assure you, Gray. She doesn't make my palms sweaty and my knees weak the way you do." His voice was low and tightened things deep within her. He always knew what to say to bring her back.

Clearing her throat, Grayson sat up straighter. "So where does that leave us?"

"I don't know."

Grayson frowned. "Derrick. I really can't do this anymore. I'm sorry. I can't go back to being some girl you fuck when you have free time on your hands. I can't be okay with knowing that you're going home to another woman every night. I just can't do it."

"Don't say that." His voice was gruff as he reached out and grabbed her arms, pulling her to him. His lips crashed down on hers, his hands tangling in her hair. He kissed her so roughly, so full of passion and desire. His tongue stroked hers, his mouth hard and demanding.

But she forced herself to pull away. "Stop it! I'm done with the mind games. I know I told you not to fall in love with me. I should have taken my own advice. I'm crazy about you, Derrick, and I want to explore this relationship, but I cannot and will not be second fiddle. You need to make up your mind. It's *now or never*. Make your damn choice."

CHAPTER 35

In the short beat of silence after her declaration, Grayson held her breath. A part of her was already resigned to the fact he was out of reach. That he would forever be a playboy, never ready to settle down or choose.

"I'll take now," he said roughly and pulled her back to him. "That's what I came here to tell you, but I'm obviously doing a poor job."

For a few stunned seconds, Grayson was speechless. Her voice trembled. "Do you really mean that?" she asked through tears. She could feel the heat of his fingertips through her clothes. "You want me, and only me?

"I've always wanted you. You terrify the hell out of me, and you're probably going to crush my soul, but I'm willing to take the risk. When I woke up in the hospital, all I could think about was how stupid I was for ignoring you just because my ego was hurt. I hated the thought of another man touching you. I was so jealous. I don't do jealous, but something about you... somehow you got so deep under my skin. I don't want to share you. I know it's selfish, but I want you all to myself."

"I don't want to share you either." Grayson threw her leg over his and straddled him on the couch, cupping his face between her hands. She could feel his arousal through his pants as his hand slid up her thigh.

His gaze didn't waver as he said, "Trust doesn't come easy to me."

"We'll have to earn each other's trust. Will you move out? End whatever it is you have going on with Megan?"

Derrick nodded, running his fingers through her hair. "I'll get my own place. You can help me pick it out."

"Will you stay the weekend here with me?" One by one Grayson undid the buttons of his shirt and pulled out the shirttails. He had on a white T-shirt underneath, and she wanted to rip it off him. She needed to feel his skin on hers.

"Definitely," Derrick replied, his voice husky.

"I'm so glad you're alive," Grayson whispered, feeling lame because the statement didn't really convey the extent of how happy she was he'd survived.

"Me, too," he murmured into her neck and pulled away to look at her. "I'm sorry I was such an ass."

Grayson drew a shaky breath and said quietly, "I've never been this afraid."

"If you weren't, I would be worried. We'll take it one day at a time. I'm sure it won't all be smooth sailing. I'll still get jealous and insecure, and we'll both doubt each other, but anything worthwhile is never easy."

She made a face. "I hope I'm enough to tame your wild ways."

Derrick laughed but sobered quickly. "I think that goes both ways. It seems like you had a little too much fun while I was gone."

Grayson didn't miss the way his body tensed. "We've both been horrible. Can't we try starting fresh? Turn over a new leaf, or whatever it is they say?"

"Do you think we really could just move on from the past?" Derrick asked, running his hands up her bare arms. "I'm worried it's this big hatchet hovering over our head, and we'll never have a real chance at moving forward."

"I think if we want this bad enough we're going to have to," Grayson said simply. "I know it won't be easy for either of us, but I'm willing to put in the effort if you are."

"More than willing."

"What do we do now?"

Derrick's lips quirked up. "As much as I hate to say it, I think we should spend time together with our clothes on and get to know each other."

"That could be fun." Grayson grinned. Her hand slipped up his T-shirt and she ran her fingers across his muscular back. "Just as long as we don't always have to keep our clothes on."

"I'm sure we can make some allowances." Derrick's hand traveled under her shirt. A moan escaped her lips. It had been way too long.

Grayson leaned down and pressed her lips to his. His kiss left her momentarily breathless. He dipped his head, trailing his hot lips down her collarbone and then down to her breast, sucking her nipple through her cotton shirt, sending a jolt between her legs. She gasped his name.

Derrick rose to his feet and pulled her gently up,

leading her to her bedroom. He pushed through the door, and she wrapped her arms around him, her chest pressed to his. She could feel his heart beating rapidly.

"Can you?" Grayson whispered.

"I can try. I might not be up to my old standards." He pulled her shirt off and tossed it on the ground reaching back to unclasp her bra.

He took a moment to stare at her, his green eyes raking slowly down her whole body as if he was memorizing every inch of her. "I don't deserve you." His gaze met hers his hands by his side.

"Shut up and kiss me," Grayson said with a smile. Their lips met again in a deep, desperate kiss that left Grayson's head spinning.

Derrick threw off his button-down shirt.

When Grayson tugged off his T-shirt, she gaped in astonishment. A pink, puckered scar about three inches thick ran down the full length of his stomach.

"Oh my god." She ran her hand down it, the baby soft skin a contrast against his rigid body.

"Flayed me open." His body was tense, and she wondered if he was self-conscious about this huge mark on his beautiful body.

"I see that. You know, scars are sexy." She tilted her head and ran her tongue along the scars on his face, then down his neck stopping to lightly kiss the pulse in the hollow of his throat. Slowly, Grayson continued down his chest and stomach to the top of his pants. She ran her hands down the full length of him.

He cleared his throat as she fumbled with the buttons of his pants. "They're everywhere. I guess that makes me extra sexy."

A. J. DENNETT

Grayson slipped his pants down his thighs, running her hands down his muscles. She paused at one of the many divots in his skin. "Does it hurt when I touch it?"

"No." He ran his hand through her hair. "I've missed you." He whispered pulling her back up and pressed his forehead to hers. The move felt so intimate and sweet. She stared into his eyes and bit the corner of her lip, suddenly shy.

Even though they'd had sex dozens of times, this felt different. She was nervous, like it was their first time. Her heart pounded in her ears, and butterflies danced in her stomach.

He trailed his finger down the side of her jaw and smiled. Her desire for him made her dizzy.

Stepping backwards, Grayson waited until she felt her bed at her shins and pulled Derrick down with her.

Propping himself up with one arms, his other hand trailed down her stomach. His fingers dipped inside and caressed her knowingly. "Jesus, Grayson I've missed the feel of you."

"Me, too." Grayson groaned trembling with need as her hips arched silently begging him to enter her.

"Come for me first." Derrick's voice was thick as his thumb circled the swollen ball of flesh. His fingers stroked her until her body tensed, and her legs shook uncontrollably. Waves of pleasure caused her mind to completely go blank. An aching emptiness filled her when he pulled his hand away.

Grayson groaned in protest.

"So greedy," Derrick whispered when she raised her hips again.

"I love you," Grayson murmured.

"Do you?" His eyes bore into hers, and watched her face when he slid slowly inside.

"Yes," Grayson moaned, enjoying the sensation of the fullness of him.

She'd been so lonely for him over the months. His lower lip brushed the curve of her ear, and silent tears fell down her cheeks. His strong forearms slid under her back, and his hand gripped her shoulders. She lifted her hips eagerly, and her hands roamed his thick arms. She felt safe and secure in his arms.

He paused and looked down at her. "And I love you, Gray."

Grayson wrapped her legs around him, pulling him closer. She couldn't seem to get close enough. So long she'd waited to hear those words from his lips.

Every thrust left Grayson gasping. Her whole body was hypersensitive. Usually when they had sex, it was fast and frantic, but this time it was slow, lingering and sweet as if they were savoring every second.

She ran her fingers across the sweat-slicked muscles of his broad shoulders and moaned into his mouth.

She never wanted to let him go. For the first time, she gave herself over completely to him. There was no holding back, no fear, just the primal need to be with him. She knew they belonged to each other. Her whole body shivered in pleasure when he brought her body to climax, again and again.

She felt so wonderfully alive in his arms. It was strange, but for some reason, when he looked into her eyes, she felt like he was really seeing her, flaws and all. What surprised her most was that he looked like he loved everything he saw.

Some time later, deeply content, Grayson laid her

head on Derrick's chest. Every muscle in her body was limp. She lay there in a haze, feeling warm and protected wrapped in his arms.

She was the first to break the silence. "You know you're the boy my mom warned me about," she told him, poking his chest playfully.

"Guy on a motorcycle?"

Grayson laughed. "A Taurus. She said I wouldn't be happy until I found one."

Derrick gave her a lopsided smile, and Grayson nuzzled him. In that moment, curled against his side, their hands meeting on his chest, she had never felt so close to another human being.

Derrick's lips touched the inside of her wrist, and she sighed softly. "I want to make you happy, Gray."

Hope and joy soared through her, though it was mixed with a touch of fear. They'd been through so much, both bad and good. There was no guarantee they'd make it, no matter how dedicated they were, but she was okay with that. She didn't know where the relationship would go exactly, but for now she was willing to enjoy the ride.

Acknowledgments

I would like to thank everyone involved in helping this book become a reality. My husband for his unwavering support. My beta readers Amy and Heather for their invaluable input. The editors Heather and Allison for their patiences with my comma issues. Eden Crane for the gorgeous cover.

About the Author

A.J. Bennett lives in Nashville, Tn with her husband and bulldog. She's addicted to coffee, popcorn and books. To find out more about A.J. checkout her website.

ajbennettauthor.com

Made in the USA
Charleston, SC
15 May 2015